D0066749

SIDDHARTHA

Hermann Hesse

Prestwick House

LITERARY TOUCHSTONE CLASSICS ™

P.O. Box 658 Clayton, Delaware 19938 • www.prestwickhouse.com

SENIOR EDITOR: Paul Moliken

EDITOR: M.A. Roberts

COVER PHOTOGRAPHY: Steve Knox

COVER ILLUSTRATION AND DESIGN: Larry Knox

PRODUCTION: Jerry Clark

Prestwick House
LITERARY TOUCHSTONE CLASSICS™

P.O. BOX 658 • CLAYTON, DELAWARE 19938
TEL: 1.800.932.4593
FAX: 1.888.718.9333
WEB: www.prestwickhouse.com

Prestwick House Teaching Units™, Activity Packs™, and Response Journals™ are the perfect complement for these editions. To purchase teaching resources for this book, visit www.prestwickhouse.com

This Prestwick House edition is an unabridged republication, with emendations, of an anonymous translation of *Siddhartha*.

ISBN 978-1-58049-390-1

SIDDHARTHA

Hermann Hesse

CONTENTS

Notes

What is a literary classic and why are these classic works important to the world?

A literary classic is a work of the highest excellence that has something important to say about life and/or the human condition and says it with great artistry. A classic, through its enduring presence, has withstood the test of time and is not bound by time, place, or customs. It speaks to us today as forcefully as it spoke to people one hundred or more years ago, and as forcefully as it will speak to people of future generations. For this reason, a classic is said to have universality.

Hermann Hesse was born in Calw, Germany, in 1877. He visited India in 1911; it was most likely this visit that formed the basis for the novel *Siddhartha*, first published in 1922. Hesse immigrated to Switzerland in 1912 and became a Swiss citizen about a decade later. He was strongly opposed to the militarism of Germany during both World Wars, and in 1943, the Nazis would not allow the publication of one of his most famous novels—*The Glass Bead Game*, which was then published in Zürich. Hesse won the Nobel Prize for literature in 1946, and wrote no other major works after receiving this prize. Hermann Hesse died in 1962.

READING POINTERS

Reading Pointers for Sharper Insights

Siddhartha is a novel about how a member of the priest class in India attains enlightenment over the course of his life. During the novel, Siddhartha becomes an ascetic, a merchant, and then a ferryman. It is important to note that, in terms of the book's chronology, Siddhartha spends much of his adult life (twenty years or more) as a merchant pursuing hedonistic pleasures. It is only later in life that he returns to the spiritual quest for enlightenment that he began as a young man. Large sections of time in Siddhartha's life are glossed over or skipped altogether during the narration.

Note the following themes and concepts that Hesse portrays and deals with as Siddhartha goes through his life experiences:

- One cannot be taught the path to enlightenment by someone else. Enlightenment can be attained only through a personal search for experiential wisdom. Paths to enlightenment can be as varied as the people who are seeking it because each journey toward that enlightenment is different.

- Endless words, teachings, and searches for knowledge can distract one from enlightenment. In addition, most worldly desires will stifle spiritual growth.

- All life and all matter is part of one unbroken, united whole. Time is an illusion, and the matter that was once non-life may become life. Existence, being, and life itself, therefore, are part of everything because all things actually exist simultaneously. If time itself is illusory, as Hesse puts forth in the novel, the young Siddhartha, searching for the divine, the older Siddhartha, feeding upon his desires, and the mature Siddhartha, living with the divine, all exist simultaneously.

- Another important element is the ironic and paradoxical nature of the book. One of *Siddhartha's* key philosophical beliefs is that wisdom cannot be transferred through words; the book, however, is using words to transfer this "wisdom" to the reader.

- At the beginning of the novel, Govinda and Siddhartha are presented as fast friends. Over the course of the story, however, their paths diverge and they pursue different goals. It is significant to see where each course takes the characters, and where they end up at the conclusion of the book.

- During the course of the novel, Siddhartha acquires many mentors and teachers. Who are these teachers? Are they teachers who would be considered typical for a person seeking spiritual enlightenment? What knowledge does each mentor pass on to Siddhartha?

FIRST PART

SIDDHARTHA

The Son of the Brahmin †

SIDDHARTHA, the handsome son of the Brahmin, the young falcon, grew up together with his friend Govinda, another Brahmin's son, in the shadow of the house, in the sun of the riverbank near the boats, in the shadow of the sala† forest, and in the shadow of the fig trees. The sun tanned his fair shoulders on the riverbank while he bathed, during the holy cleansing, at the holy sacrifices. Shadows flowed into his black eyes in the mango grove, during the boyish games, when his mother sang, at the holy sacrifices, during the teaching of his father the scholar, and when speaking with the wise ones. For a long time Siddhartha had taken part in the wise ones' discussions; he had practiced word-wrestling with Govinda, had practiced the art of contemplation and the duty of meditation with Govinda. He already understood how to speak the "Om"† silently, that word of words, how to speak it silently in his inner being as he inhaled, how to pronounce it silently out of himself as he exhaled, how to do so with his whole soul while his forehead was enveloped by the radiance of the clear-thinking mind. He already understood how to recognize Atman† within this inner essence of his that was indestructible and one with the universe.

Joy sprang up in his father's heart over the son who was so apt to learn and so thirsty after knowledge; he saw growing within him a great sage and priest, a prince among the Brahmins.

---

†Terms marked in the text with (†) can be looked up in the Glossary for additional information.

13

Delight welled up in his mother's heart when she saw him taking long strides, saw him sitting down and standing up: Siddhartha the strong and handsome, who strode upon lean legs and who greeted her with impeccable manners.

All the young daughters of the Brahmins felt love stirring within their hearts when Siddhartha walked through the side-streets of the city with a beaming face, a lean physique, and a royal look in his eyes.

Govinda, the Brahmin's son, however, loved him more than all of these. He loved the eye of Siddhartha and his sweet voice, his gait and the perfection of his movements; he loved everything that Siddhartha did and said, and above all he loved Siddhartha's mind, his sublime and fiery thoughts, his blazing will, and Siddhartha's high calling. Govinda knew that this would be no ordinary Brahmin, no lazy official presiding over the sacrifices, no money-grubbing merchant hawking magic trinkets, no vain and vacuous speaker, no wicked and lying priest, and also not a good-hearted but dim-witted sheep in the plebian herds. Govinda didn't want to be such a person either, didn't want to be a Brahmin like all the ten thousand other Brahmins. He wanted to follow Siddhartha, who was beloved and majestic. When Siddhartha first became a god, when he entered into the radiance, then Govinda wanted to follow him as his friend, his escort, his servant, his spear-carrier, and his shadow.

In this manner, everyone loved Siddhartha. He brought everyone joy; he pleased everyone.

However, Siddhartha didn't bring himself joy; he didn't please himself. He strolled on the rosy paths of the fig gardens, sat in the blue shadows of the grove of meditation, washed his limbs daily in baths of atonement, and sacrificed in the deep shadows of the mango forest. Everyone loved him; he was joyous to them, and yet he carried no joy in his own heart. Dreams and restless thoughts came flowing to him out of the river's water, twinkled to him from the stars of the night, melted out of the sunbeams. Dreams and anxiety came billowing out of the sacrificial smoke, whispering from the verses of the Rig-Veda,[†] or trickling out of the old Brahmin's teachings.

Siddhartha had started to cultivate the seed of discontent within himself. He had started to feel as if his father's love, his mother's love, and the love of his friend Govinda wouldn't make him happy forever, wouldn't bring him peace, satisfy him, and be sufficient for all time. He had started to suspect that his illustrious father, his other teachers, and the wise Brahmins had shared the majority and the best of their wisdom with him, that they had already poured their all into his ready vessel without filling the vessel: the mind wasn't satisfied, the soul wasn't quiet, the heart wasn't stilled. The purifications were nice, but they were just water, and didn't wash away sins; they didn't cure the mental thirst or allay his heart's anxiety. Sacrifices and invocations to the gods were superb—but were they sufficient? Did the sacrifices bring happiness? And what about all those gods? Was Prajapati† really the one who had created the world? Wasn't it Atman, He who was the Only One, the All-One? Weren't the gods creatures, created just as you and I were: subject to time and transitory? Was it even good, was it right, did it make sense or was it important to sacrifice to the gods? To whom else would one sacrifice, to whom else should one bring worship other than Him, the Only, the Atman? And where could Atman be found, where did he live, where did his eternal heart beat—where else other than in the self, in one's inner being, in the indestructible part of all persons that they carried within themselves? But where was this self, where was this inner being, this most paramount thing? It was not made of flesh or the legs that carried it, it wasn't just the thoughts or the awareness—or so taught the wisest men. Where then was it? One had to penetrate that far into the self, into myself, into the Atman—was there some other way, however, a search which still yielded worthwhile results? Ah, but nobody pointed to this way, nobody knew it: not father, not the teachers and wise ones, not the holy chants sung during sacrifices! They knew everything, those Brahmins and their holy books. They knew everything, they had concerned themselves with everything and with more than everything: the creation of the world, the origins of language, of foods, of inhalation and exhalation, the institution of the senses, the deeds of the gods—they knew an inordinate amount, and yet was it worthwhile to know everything like this when one didn't know the one and only thing that was most important—that which alone was important?

To be sure, many verses from the holy books—especially the Upanishads† of the Sama-Veda†—spoke about these innermost and most important things—majestic verses. "Your soul is the whole world" was written there; it was also written that the person who slept in the deepest slumber went within to his or her innermost place and lived in Atman. Wonderful wisdom stood within these verses, all the wisdom of the wisest was gathered there in the magical words, pure like the honey gathered by the bees. No, the behemoth of knowledge that innumerable generations of wise Brahmins had gathered and protected there wasn't to be lightly esteemed. But where were the Brahmins, where were the priests, the wise ones and the penitents—those who were successful not only in knowing this deepest wisdom but also in living it? Where were the elders who could merge this Atman of their dreams with the waking being, to bring it fully into their lives and into their words and deeds? Siddhartha knew many venerable Brahmins—not the least of whom was his father, who was pure, scholarly, and highly esteemed. His father was admirable: his habits were quiet and elegant, his life pure, his words wise, and the thoughts that inhabited his brow were both fine and noble—but did he who possessed so much wisdom live a blessed life? Did he have joy; wasn't he also a mere seeker, one who had thirst? Did not he, who had thirst, have to receive a holy quenching of this thirst by drinking time and time again at the sacrifices, at the books, at the conversations of the Brahmins? Why did he, who was irreproachable, have to wash out his sins every day, have to expend great effort once more to attain purification each and every day. Wasn't Atman in him; didn't the ancient spring flow in his heart? The ancient spring must be found in one's own self; one must own it! Everything else was just a search, a detour; it was to go astray.

Thus went Siddhartha's thoughts; this was his thirst, his sorrow.

He often spoke to himself out of the Chandogya-Upanishad: "Verily, the name of the Brahman† is Satyam†— in truth, one who knows this enters daily into the heavenly world." This heavenly world often appeared close, but he had never totally reached it; never had he quenched the ultimate thirst. Furthermore, among all the wise ones whom he knew whose teaching he had savored—even the wisest—among them all there were none who had totally reached the heavenly world, who had completely quenched the eternal thirst.

"Govinda," said Siddhartha to his friend, "Govinda, beloved, come with me among the Banyan trees, and we will practice meditating."

They went to the Banyan trees and sat down: here Siddhartha, and Govinda twenty paces further. When Siddhartha sat down, ready to speak the Om, he murmured and repeated the verse:

> "Om is the bow; the arrow is the soul,
> The Brahman is the arrow's goal
> That one should continuously hit."

When the usual time for practicing meditation had passed, Govinda rose up. The twilight had come, and it was time to perform the cleansing of the evening hour. He called Siddhartha's name. Siddhartha gave no answer. Siddhartha sat with his eyes open, immersed, staring with his eyes fixed upon a very far goal; the tip of his tongue stuck out a little between his teeth, and he didn't appear to be breathing. Thus he sat, shrouded in meditation, thinking Om, his soul sent out like an arrow after the Brahman.

Once, the Samanas† pulled through Siddhartha's town. They were pilgrims and ascetics: three scraggly, worn-out men who were neither old nor young, with dusty and bloody shoulders. They were nearly naked, singed by the sun, given over to loneliness, strangers and enemies of the world, and estranged, gaunt jackals in the domain of mankind. From behind them wafted a hot scent of quiet passion, of a duty that destroys, of a merciless self-effacing.

In the evening, after the hour of contemplation, Siddhartha said to Govinda: "Early tomorrow, my friend, Siddhartha will go to the Samanas. He will become a Samana."

Govinda paled when he heard these words and saw the resolution in the stony face of his friend, a resolution that, like the swiftest arrow let loose from the bow, could never be deflected. As soon as Govinda glimpsed this, he recognized: now it begins; now Siddhartha goes his own way, now his fate begins to sprout, and with his, mine. Govinda paled like the peel of a dry banana.

"O Siddhartha," he called, "Will your father allow you to do that?"

Siddhartha glanced at his friend like one just waking up. As quickly as the arrow flies, he read Govinda's soul; he read the anxiety and the devotion there.

"O Govinda," he said quietly, "don't waste any words on this. Tomorrow at daybreak I will begin a Samana's life. Don't discuss this any more."

Siddhartha stepped in the chamber where his father sat on a raffia mat, and walked behind his father, standing there until his father sensed that someone was standing behind him. The Brahmin spoke: "Is that you, Siddhartha? Well, say what you have come here to say."

Siddhartha spoke: "With your permission, my father. I have come to say to you that I am desirous of leaving your house tomorrow and going to the ascetics. My wish is to become a Samana. May my father not be opposed to this."

The Brahmin was silent, and silent so long that in the little window the stars wandered and changed their configuration before the silence in the chamber found an end. Silent and still, the son stood with crossed arms; silent and still, the father sat on the mat, and the stars moved in the heavens. Then the father spoke: "It is not fitting for the Brahmins to speak with severe and scornful words. Yet, I see displeasure moving your heart. I would not like to hear this request come out of your mouth a second time."

Slowly the Brahmin raised himself, Siddhartha, mute and with crossed arms, stood there.

"What are you waiting for?" asked the father.

Spoke Siddhartha: "You know what for."

Displeased, the father went out of the chamber; displeased, he sought his bed and lay down.

After an hour during which no sleep came to his eyes, the Brahmin stood up, paced to and fro, and stepped out of the house. Through the little window of the chamber he looked in, and saw that Siddhartha stood there with crossed arms, unmoved. His lightweight outer garment shimmered with a pale light. Restless at heart, the father returned to his bed.

After an hour during which no sleep came to his eyes, the Brahmin stood up again, paced to and fro, stepped in front of the house, and saw the moon, which had risen. Through the window of the chamber he glanced inside: there stood Siddhartha, unmoved, with crossed arms and the moonlight mirrored on his bare shins. The father, concerned in his heart, sought his bed.

And he came again after an hour, and came again after two hours; he glanced through the little window, saw Siddhartha standing in the moonlight, in the star shine, and in the darkness. And the father silently came again from hour to hour, glanced in the chamber, saw the immobile person standing there, then filled his heart with rage, filled his heart with disquietude, filled his heart with anxiety, and filled it with sorrow.

And in the last hour of the night, before the day began, he turned again, came into the chamber, and saw standing there the young boy that now appeared so large and strange to him.

"Siddhartha," said he, "What are you waiting for?"

"You know what for."

"Will you always stand like this and wait, until it becomes day, becomes noon, becomes evening?"

"I will stand and wait."

"You will become tired, Siddhartha."

"I will become tired."

"You will fall asleep, Siddhartha."

"I will not fall asleep."

"You will die, Siddhartha."

"I will die."

"And you would rather die than listen to your father?"

"Siddhartha has always listened to his father."

"So you want to give up your intentions?"

"Siddhartha will do what his father is going to tell him to do."

The first sunshine of the day fell upon the chamber. The Brahmin saw that Siddhartha's knees were gently trembling. In Siddhartha's face, however, he saw no trembling: the eyes looked far away. Then the father realized that Siddhartha had already gone from him and his household, that he had already left him.

The father touched Siddhartha's shoulder.

"You will," he said, "go in the woods and be a Samana. If you have found blessedness in the woods, then come and teach me how to be blessed. If you find disappointment, then return once more and let us once again sacrifice to the gods together. Now go and kiss your mother; tell her where you are going. For me, however, it is time to go to the river and perform the first cleansing."

He took his hand from his son's shoulder and went outside. Siddhartha swayed to one side as if he wanted to go. He conquered his limbs, bowed down before his father and went to his mother in order to do as his father had said.

At dawn, he slowly and with stiff legs left the still-quiet city. At the last hut, he saw a shadow that was crouching down there rise up and join him, the new pilgrim—Govinda.

"You have come," said Siddhartha as he smiled.

"I have come," said Govinda.

With the Samanas

T HEY CAUGHT UP with the ascetics, the scraggly Samanas, in the evening of that same day, and they offered to accompany them and obey them. They were accepted.

Siddhartha gave his robe as a gift to a poor Brahmin along the road. Siddhartha wore only a loincloth and an unstitched, earth-colored shawl. He ate only once a day, and never ate anything cooked. He fasted for fifteen days. He fasted for twenty-eight days. The flesh on his thighs and cheeks dwindled away. From his enlarged eyes flickered hot dreams; the nails grew long on his dried-out fingers and he had a dry, unkempt beard on his chin. When he encountered females, his gaze was frigid; when he went through a city where the men were handsomely clothed, his mouth twitched with contempt. He saw merchants conduct trade, princes go on their hunts, mourners bemoan deaths, whores offer their services, doctors tend to their sick, priests specify which days were good for sowing seed, lovers love, mothers shush their children—and nothing was worth even the glance of his eyes. Everything was a lie, everything stank, everything stank of lies, everything feigned meaning and happiness and beauty, and yet everything was decaying while nobody acknowledged the fact. The world tasted bitter; life was agony.

One goal loomed before Siddhartha, and only one: to become empty, to be empty of thirst, of wishing, of dreams—empty of all joy and pain. He wanted the Self to die, to no longer be an "I," to find peace with an empty heart. His goal was to stand open to the wonder of thoughts conceived in self-dissolution. When every shred of his self had been conquered and put to death, when every longing and every inclination of the heart had been silenced, then the Ultimate had to awaken, that which was innermost had to come into being, that which was nothing less than the ego, the great secret.

Siddhartha stood silently in the intense rays streaming vertically from the sun; blazing with pain and blazing with thirst, he stood until he felt neither pain nor thirst any longer. He stood silently in the rain while water dripped from his hair over his frozen shoulders, over his frigid hips and legs, and still the penitent stood there until his shoulders and legs were frozen no longer, until they became silent and were still. Silently he crouched down among the briar tendrils, while blood dripped from his burning skin and pus came from his lesions. Siddhartha languished there without movement or any animation until the blood flowed no longer, until he felt nothing stinging or burning any more.

Siddhartha sat upright and learned how to breathe sparingly, learned how to get by with little breath and then learned how to halt his breathing. He learned, beginning with the breath, how to quiet his heartbeat, and then how to diminish his heart's beating until it was very little and then was almost nonexistent.

Under the teaching of the oldest Samanas, Siddhartha mastered self-denial, practiced mystic contemplation according to the new methods of the Samanas. A heron flew over the bamboo forest—and Siddhartha took the heron into his soul, he flew over the woods and the mountains. He was a heron: he fed upon fish and hungered with the heron's hunger, he spoke the cawing of the heron and died the heron's death. A dead jackal lay there on the sandy riverbank, and Siddhartha's soul slipped into the dead body. He was a dead jackal: he lay on the beach, he swelled up and stank, he rotted away and was dismembered by the hyenas before being skinned by the vultures. He turned to a skeleton and then to dust, and then he blew into the fields. And Siddhartha's soul returned. His soul had died, it had decayed, it had crumbled to dust. He had tasted the hazy intoxication of the cycle of existence and, like the hunter poised for the opportunity, awaited his chance to escape from this cycle to the place where causality ended and an eternity free of sorrow began. He deadened his senses and dulled his memory, he slid out of his self-existence into a thousand strange created things: he was an animal, he was carrion, he was stone, wood, and water, and every time when he found himself awakened once more, whether the sun or moon was shining, he was once more himself within the cycle of existence. He felt thirst, he overcame his thirst, and then he felt new thirst.

With the Samanas, Siddhartha learned quite a bit, and learned how to go away from the self in many ways. He followed the method of self-dissolution through pain, whereby he suffered voluntarily and overcame the pain, hunger, thirst, or fatigue. He achieved self-dissolution through meditation, by the concentrated clearing of all perceptions from his senses. He learned to go by these ways as well as others: he abandoned his being a thousand times, he lingered in the Not-Self hours and days at a time. But, although these paths led away from one's being, in the end they always led back to the self. Although Siddhartha fled the self a thousand times and tarried in nothing, although he spent time within animals and stones, the return was unavoidable. The hours where he found his own being were inescapable, whether in shadows or in rain he was once more Siddhartha, and the agony of the cycle of existence was once again laid upon him.

Govinda, his shadow, lived by his side. He followed this same path and he himself undertook the same tasks. They seldom spoke more to one another than the service and practices required. At times, these two went through the villages so that they could beg sustenance for themselves and their teachers.

"What do you think, Govinda?" said Siddhartha once during these begging trips, "What do you think? Should we go further? Have we achieved our goal?"

Govinda answered: "We have learned, and we continue to learn. You will be a great Samana, Siddhartha. You have learned every practice quickly, and the old Samanas have often marveled at you. One day, you will be a saint, Siddhartha."

Siddhartha spoke: "It doesn't look that way to me, my friend. The things that I have learned with the Samanas up to this point, O Govinda, I could have learned even easier and more quickly. I could have learned it in any pub located in the whore's district, there among the manual laborers and the gamblers, my friend."

Govinda said: "Siddhartha is joking with me! How could you have acquired meditation, and how could you have learned how to cease breathing; how could you have possessed immunity to hunger and pain there among all that is miserable?"

And Siddhartha spoke quietly, as if to himself: "What is mystic contemplation? What is an out-of-body experience? What is fasting? What is the cessation of breath? It is flight from one's being, it's a brief escape out of the agony of self-existence, it's a momentary anesthetic against the pain and meaninglessness of life. The ox driver could find this selfsame flight. He could find the very same momentary anesthetic in the tavern when he drinks a couple of bowls of rice wine or fermented coconut milk. At that point he no longer senses his self. He finds fleeting anesthesia. He, while

falling into slumber over his bowl of rice wine, finds the same thing that
Siddhartha and Govinda find when they, after hours of practice, are able
to journey outside of their bodies. So it is, O Govinda."

Govinda spoke: "So you say, O friend, but you know that Siddhartha
is no ox driver and that a Samana is no drunkard. True, the drinker finds
anesthesia, true he finds short flight and respite, but he returns out of the
illusion and finds everything just as it was before; he has not grown wiser,
he has not gathered knowledge, he has not climbed one step higher."

And Siddhartha said, smiling: "I don't know that I'm never going to
become a drunkard. I only know that I, Siddhartha, only find momentary
numbness in my methods and meditations. I know that I am even as far
removed from wisdom and deliverance as the child is while still cradled by
the mother's love. This I know, O Govinda; this I know."

At another time when Siddhartha and Govinda left the woods in order
to beg for some nourishment for their brothers and teachers in a village,
Siddhartha began to speak, saying: "How now, Govinda; are we truly on
the right path? Are we really growing towards a realization? Or are we,
perhaps, just going in circles—we who think that at some point we shall
escape the circle of existence?"

Govinda said: "We have learned much, Siddhartha, and much remains
to be learned. We're not going in circles; we are going upwards. The circle
is a spiral, and we have already climbed several steps."

Siddhartha answered: "How old do you think our oldest Samana, the
one most worthy of honor, really is?"

Said Govinda: "The oldest among us is perhaps sixty years."

And Siddhartha: "He is sixty years old and has never reached Nirvana.
He will become seventy and eighty, and you and I will also become old
while practicing, fasting, and meditating. But we will not reach Nirvana
just as he will not. O Govinda, I believe that, among all the Samanas in
existence, not even a single one will reach Nirvana. We may find consola-
tion, or numbness, or may learn genuine skills with which we can deceive
ourselves. But the fundamental thing, that Way of Ways, we do not find."

"On the contrary," said Govinda, "you should not speak such outra-
geous words, Siddhartha! Are you saying we will find no Way of Ways
among so many learned men, Brahmins, and seekers, among so many
sincerely zealous and holy men, or among so many strong and venerable
Samanas?

Siddhartha then said in a voice that contained scoffing and sadness,
in a voice that was quiet, somewhat sad, and somewhat mocking: "Soon,
Govinda, your friend will leave the Samanas' path that he has traveled for
so long with you. Unfortunately, I thirst, O Govinda, and on this long

path of the Samana my thirst had dwindled until it has become nothing. I have always thirsted after enlightenment; I am always becoming full of questions. I have asked the Brahmins and the holy Vedas year after year. O Govinda, perhaps it would have been just as good, just as intelligent, and just as efficacious if I had asked the rhinoceros birds or the chimpanzees. It has required a great deal of time, and even now I have not come to the end of the journey of learning this fact, O Govinda: that man can learn nothing! The thing that we call "learning" is, in truth, nonexistent! It is inherent, oh my friend, in a knowledge that is everywhere, that is Atman; it is in me and in you and in every essence. I am starting to believe that this knowledge has no more aggressive enemy than learning and the desire for knowledge.

Govinda remained on the road, standing there. He raised his hands and said: "You shouldn't alarm your friend with such conversations! Your words truly stir up worry within my heart. Just think: what would lend holiness to one's prayers, what would make the Brahmin class worthy of honor, what would make the Samanas holy, if, as you say, there is no learning?! What would all of these be, O Siddhartha, in such a case; what would be holy, what would be worthwhile, what would be venerable?

Govinda then murmured a verse out of the Upanishad:

"Whosoever immerses themselves in Atman through contemplation and a purified spirit.
Will receive ineffable blessing in their heart."

Siddhartha, however, remained silent. He thought about the words Govinda had spoken to him, and considered them until their conclusion.

Yes, he thought while he stood there with a lowered head, what still remains of it all; what appears holy to us? What remains? What is worth doing? He then shook his head.

One time, when both lads had lived with the Samanas and shared their practices for about three years, a rumor, an adage arrived to them through various highways and byways: one named "Gotama" has appeared, the sublime, the Buddha, who has overcome the world's anguish within himself and has brought the Wheel of Rebirth to a standstill. He was surrounded by disciples as he went through the land, teaching. He was without possessions, homeless, womanless, wearing the yellow mantle of an ascetic but with a cheerful visage. He was a saint; princes and Brahmins bowed down before him and wanted to sit under his tutelage.

This tale, this rumor, this fairy tale resonated outwards, wafted upwards, and traveled here and there. The Brahmins spoke about these things in the cities, the Samanas did so in the woods; the name of Gotama, the Buddha, hammered upon the ears of young lads time and time again. They heard both good and bad reports about Gotama; they heard both adulation and abuse.

Just as it is in a land where the pestilence is raging, and tidings go forth: "here or there is a man, a sage, a harbinger whose words or whose breath, when they fell upon a person, were sufficient for healing the plague"—and just as every person spoke about these reports running rampant throughout in the land, with many believing and doubting while others immediately went on their way to seek help from the wise man—in this same way went out every tale and aromatic report of Gotama, the Buddha, the wise man of the Sakya clan. According to the believers, he possessed the highest knowledge: he could recall his previous lives, he had reached Nirvana and would not return time and again to the circle of existence, he did not submerge himself any longer in the turbulent streams of mortal beings. Many majestic and unbelievable things were reported of him: he had done miracles, he had overcome the devil, he had spoken with the gods. His enemies and the unbelievers, however, said that this Gotama was a vain seducer. They said he lived extravagantly, that he despised the sacrifices, that he had no learning and had intimate knowledge of neither customs nor the caste† system.

The tales of the Buddha sounded sweet; the reports had the scent of magic. The world was certainly sick, and life was difficult to endure—and see, here a fountain appeared to spring up, here a clarion call appeared to sound that was trustworthy, mild, and full of elegant promises. Everywhere that the rumor of the Buddha cropped up, in every place in the lands of India the lads pricked up their ears. They felt a deep longing of the heart; they felt hope. Among the sons of the Brahmin and in every city and village a pilgrim or a stranger was welcome when he brought news of him who was Sublime, the Sakyamuni.

The tales slowly permeated to the Samanas in the woods as well as to Siddhartha and Govinda. The tales came slowly; they trickled in drops that were heavy with hope and heavy with doubt. They spoke little about these things, as the oldest Samana was no friend of these tales. He had heard that the one everyone looked upon as the Buddha had previously been an ascetic in the woods but had turned back to pursue luxury and the world's lusts, and he had little regard for this Gotama.

"O Siddhartha," Govinda said at one point to his friend, "Today I was in the village, and a Brahmin invited me to step into his house. In his house was a Brahmin's son from Magadha who had seen the Buddha with his own eyes and had heard his teachings. Truly, the breath in my breast failed me, and I thought to myself: how I would also like—how I would like us both,

Siddhartha and I, to experience the hour when we would hear the teachings proceed from the mouth of this perfect one! Speak, friend, don't we
want to go there and listen to the teachings that come from the Buddha's
mouth?"

Siddhartha said: "I had always thought, O Govinda, that you would
remain with the Samanas. I have always believed that it was your goal
to become sixty or seventy years old, pursuing all the while the methods
and means that adorn the Samanas. Ah, but see, I had known too little
of Govinda. I had known little of your true heart! Now, all right—as you
wish, most precious one: open forth a path and go ahead on it. Go where
the Buddha proclaims his teachings."

Govinda said: "You love to mock it. You shall mock it regardless,
Siddhartha! Don't you also desire, doesn't a yearning also awaken within
you to hear this teaching? Didn't you once say to me that it wouldn't be
long before you left the way of the Samanas?"

Siddhartha laughed at this; he laughed and his voice took on a shadow
of sorrow and mockery. He said: "Truly, Govinda, you have spoken truly
and have remembered correctly. Would that you had remembered the
other things you have heard me say as well, namely that I have become
skeptical and tired about teaching and learning, and that my trust in words
that come from teachers is small. But nevertheless, dear one, I am ready
to hear every teaching—even though I in my heart believe that we have
already gleaned the best fruit from every teaching."

Govinda spoke: "Your readiness to do so strikes joy in my heart. But
say, how is that possible? How could the teaching of Gotama have already
developed its best fruit before we have ever examined it?"

Siddhartha said: "Let's savor this fruit and save the rest of it for later,
Govinda! We already owe the Gotama thanks for this fruit, however, and
it lies in the fact that he is calling us away from the Samanas! Whether he
has other things to give us, O friend…well, let us wait for this with quieted
hearts."

On this same day, Siddhartha gave the oldest Samana his decision:
that he would leave. He let the elder know with the politeness and decorum that was fitting for disciples and scholars. The Samana, however,
approached him in scorn because both of the lads were leaving. He spoke
loudly and used coarse insults.

Govinda was shocked and became embarrassed. Siddhartha, however,
leaned his mouth over to Govinda's ear and whispered to him "Now I will
show the old one that I have learned something from him."

At this Siddhartha took up a position in front of the Samana and
gathered his thoughts. He captured the elder's gaze with his own,

entranced him, made him be silent, and drained him of his will. Siddhartha conquered the elder's will, making the elder do what he wanted. The old man became silent as his eyes stared; he was paralyzed and his arms hung down. The feeble elder was shot out of the sky by Siddhartha's spellbinding. Siddhartha's thoughts seized hold of the Samana and had to perform the actions imposed upon him. So the elder bowed down several times, completing this blessed gesture fully, and then stammered a devout wish for good travels. The lads reciprocated this wish, likewise bowing down with thanks as they walked away and bid him farewell.

As they went on their way, Govinda said: "O Siddhartha, you have learned more among the Samanas than I knew. It is very difficult indeed to bewitch an older Samana. Had you remained there, you truly would have learned to walk on water before too long."

"I don't have any desire to walk on water," said Siddhartha. "Let the old Samanas satisfy themselves with such tricks."

Gotama

EVERY CHILD IN the town of Savathi knew the name of the exalted Buddha, and every house was prepared to fill the alms-dishes of the silent beggars who were Gotama's disciples. Gotama's favorite place to stay was near the town: the grove of Jetavana. The wealthy merchant Anathapindika, an obedient worshipper of the exalted one, had given this grove as a gift to Gotama and his people

As the two young ascetics had searched for Gotama's dwelling place, the responses and the stories they had heard pointed them towards this area. Upon arriving in Savathi, they received a meal at the door of the first house where they had stood and begged. Siddhartha asked the woman who gave them the meal:

"You whose deeds are most gracious—we would be most glad to learn where the Buddha, who is venerable, spends his time. We are two Samanas from the woods, and have come in order to see him who is the perfected one, and to hear the teachings from his mouth."

The woman said: "You Samanas from the forest have certainly come to the right place. Know this: it is in Jetavana, in the garden of Anathapindika, that the Sublime one spends his time. You should spend the night there, pilgrims, because there is enough room there for the countless multitudes who flock here to hear the teachings from his mouth."

Govinda rejoiced at this, and full of joy he exclaimed: "Well then, our goal has been reached and our path has come to an end! But tell us, you who are mother to the pilgrims, do you know him, the Buddha; have you seen him with your eyes?"

Spoke the woman: "Many times have I seen him who is sublime. I have seen him upon many occasions, how he goes silently through the alleyways in a yellow mantle, how he silently extends his bowl at the doors of houses, and how he carries the filled dish away."

Govinda listened with delight, and still wanted to ask and hear about many things. But Siddhartha was in a hurry to continue onwards. They thanked her and went on their way, hardly having to ask for directions because so many pilgrims and monks from Gotama's neighborhood were on their way to Jetavana. As they reached it that evening, there were constant arrivals, with people shouting or talking as they sought shelter and received it. The two Samanas, who were used to living in the forest, silently and quickly found a place to stay and rested there until the morning.

At sunrise, they were astounded to see such large throngs of believers and people who were curious who had spent the night there. Monks went to and fro in yellow robes on all the paths of the majestic grove; they sat here and there among the trees, immersed in contemplation or spiritual discussions. The shadowy gardens were like a city, full of people who were bustling like bees. Most of the monks went with their alms-dishes to collect food in the city for the midday meal, the only meal of the day. The Buddha himself, the enlightened one, was also in the habit of taking this walk to beg in the morning.

Siddhartha recognized him as soon as he saw him, as if a god had pointed him out to him. He saw him, a simple man in a yellow robe, bearing the alms-dish in his hand, walking silently.

"See here!" Siddhartha said quietly to Govinda. "This one here is the Buddha."

Attentively, Govinda glanced at the monk in the yellow robe, who seemed no different from the hundreds of other monks. And soon, Govinda also realized: this is the one. And they followed him and observed him.

The Buddha went on his way, modestly and deep in his thoughts, his calm face was neither happy nor sad, it seemed to smile quietly and inwardly. With his hidden smile, the Buddha strolled on quietly, calmly, and not unlike a healthy child. He wore his robe and placed his feet much as all the other monks did, according to an exact rule. But his face and his gait, his gaze lowered quietly, his motionless hands hanging down, and even every finger of his dangling hands bespoke peace, expressed perfection—they did not search, or imitate—as they breathed softly with a calm that did not wither, with a light that did not fade, and with a peace that was intangible.

In this way Gotama strolled towards the town collecting alms, and the two Samanas recognized him simply by the perfection of his peace, by the

stillness of his being in which there was no seeking, no desire, no imita-
tion, no attempts at being seen—only light and peace.

"Today, we'll hear the teachings from his mouth." said Govinda.

Siddhartha gave no answer. He was slightly curious about this teaching. He did not believe that they would teach him anything new, but he,
like Govinda, had heard the contents of this Buddha's teachings again and
again, though these reports only represented second- or third-hand information. But attentively he looked at Gotama's head, his shoulders, his feet,
his quietly dangling hand, and it seemed to Siddhartha as if every joint of
every finger of this hand was a teacher who spoke, breathed of, exhaled
the fragrance of, and shone forth with truth. This man, this Buddha was
truthful down to the gesture of his last finger. This man was holy. Never
before had Siddhartha revered a person so much, never before had he loved
a person as much as this one.

They both followed the Buddha until they reached the town and then
returned in silence, for they themselves had thought to abstain from food
for the day. They saw Gotama returning—what he ate could not even have
satisfied a bird's appetite—and they saw him retiring into the shade of the
mango trees.

But in the evening, when the heat cooled down and everyone in the
camp started to bustle about and gathered around, they heard the Buddha
teaching. They heard his voice, and it also was perfected, wholly calm and
full of peace. Gotama taught the lessons of suffering, of the origin of suffering, of ways to relieve suffering. Calmly and clearly his quiet speech flowed
on. Suffering was life, the whole world was full of suffering, but salvation
from suffering had been found: salvation was obtained by walking the path
of the Buddha. The exalted one spoke with a voice that was soft yet firm; he
taught the four main doctrines and taught the eightfold path. He patiently
followed the typical path of teaching by using examples and repetition; his
voice hovered brightly and quietly over the listeners like a light, like a star
in heaven.

Night had already fallen when the Buddha had ended his speech, and
many pilgrims stepped forward and asked to be accepted into the community, taking their refuge in his teachings. And Gotama accepted them
by saying: "You have heard the teachings well, they have come to you well.
Join us then and walk in holiness, putting an end to all suffering."

Behold, then Govinda, the shy one, also stepped forward and spoke: "I
also take my refuge in the exalted one and his teachings," and he asked to
be accepted into the community of discipleship and was accepted.

Directly after this, when the Buddha had retired for the night, Govinda
turned to Siddhartha and spoke eagerly: "Siddhartha, it is not my place to

reproach you. We have both heard the exalted one, we have both heard the teachings. Govinda has heard the teachings, he has taken refuge in it. But you, my honored friend, don't you also want to walk the path of salvation? Would you want to hesitate, do you want to wait any longer?"

Siddhartha awakened as if he had been asleep, when he heard Govinda's words. For a long time, he looked into Govinda's face. Then he spoke quietly, in a voice without mockery: "Govinda, my friend, now you have taken this step, you have chosen this path. You've always been my friend, O Govinda; you've always walked one step behind me. Often have I thought: Won't Govinda for once also take a step by himself, without me, out of his own soul? Behold, now you've turned into a man and are choosing your path for yourself. May you follow it to the end, O my friend! May you find salvation!"

Govinda, who had not yet fully understood, repeated his question in an impatient tone: "Speak up, I beg you, dear one! Tell me, since it could not be any other way, that you also, my erudite friend, will take your refuge in the exalted Buddha!"

Siddhartha placed his hand on Govinda's shoulder: "You failed to hear my blessing for you, O Govinda. I'm repeating it: May you follow this path to its end; may you find salvation!"

In this instant, Govinda realized that his friend had left him, and he started to weep.

"Siddhartha!" he exclaimed in a lamenting voice.

Siddhartha spoke kindly to him: "Don't forget, Govinda, that you are now one of the Samanas of the Buddha! You have renounced your home and your parents, renounced your heritage and possessions, renounced your free will, renounced all friendship. This is what the teachings require, this is what the exalted one wants. This is what you wanted for yourself. Tomorrow, O Govinda, I'll leave you."

For a long time, the friends continued walking in the grove; for a long time, they lay there and found no sleep. And over and over again, Govinda urged his friend to tell him why he didn't want to seek refuge in Gotama's teachings, what fault he had found in them. But Siddhartha turned him away every time and said: "Be at peace, Govinda! The teachings of the sublime one are very good; how could I find an error in them?"

Very early in the morning, a follower of Buddha, one of his oldest monks, went through the garden and called to him all those who had taken their refuge in the teachings and become novices, so that he could lay the yellow robe on them and instruct them in the primary teachings and duties of their position. Then Govinda tore himself away, embraced once again his childhood friend, and left with the novices.

But Siddhartha walked through the grove, lost in thought. There he encountered Gotama, the exalted one, and as he greeted him with respect and the Buddha's glance was so full of kindness and calm, the young man summoned his courage and asked the venerable one for the permission to speak to him. Silently the exalted one nodded his assent.

Spoke Siddhartha: "Yesterday, O exalted one, it was my privilege to hear your wondrous teachings. I came here from afar with my friend to hear your teachings. And now my friend is going to remain with your people; he has taken his refuge with you. I, however, will begin my pilgrimage once again."

"As you please," said the revered one politely.

"My speech is too bold," continued Siddhartha, "but I do not want to leave the exalted one without having honestly shared with him my thoughts. Does it please the venerable one to listen to me for one moment longer?"

Silently, the Buddha nodded his assent.

Siddhartha said: "There is one thing, O most venerable one, that I have admired in your teachings most of all. Everything in your teachings is perfectly clear and proven; you are presenting the world as a perfect chain, a chain which is never and nowhere broken, an eternal chain, the links of which are causes and effects. Never before has this been so clearly seen; never before has this been presented so irrefutably. Truly, the heart of every Brahmin has to beat stronger with love, once he has seen the world connected perfectly through your teachings, without gaps, clear as a crystal, not depending on chance or upon gods. Whether it may be good or bad, whether living according to it would be suffering or joy, may remain undecided. It may be that this is not essential. However, the unity of the world, the interconnectedness of all that transpires, the fact that the great and the small things are all encompassed by the same forces of time and law of causation, of coming into being and of dying—these shine brightly out of your exalted teachings, O perfected one. But according to your very own teachings, this unity and logical consistency of all things is nevertheless broken in one place. But through a small gap this world of unity is invaded by something alien, something which had not been there before, and which cannot be demonstrated and cannot be proven: these are your teachings of overcoming the world, of salvation. But with this small gap, with this small breach, the entire eternal and uniform law of the world is being smashed to pieces and is done away with. Please forgive me for expressing this objection."

Quietly, Gotama had listened to him, unmoved. Now the perfected one spoke with his kind, polite, and clear voice: "You've heard the teachings, O son of a Brahmin, and it is good that you've thought about them deeply. You've found a gap in them, a mistake. You should think about this further. Let me warn you, however, O seeker of knowledge, of the thicket of opinions and of arguing about words. Opinions are insubstantial: they may be beautiful or ugly, smart or foolish; everyone can support them or discard them. But the teachings you've heard from me are not my opinions, and their goal is not to explain the world to those who seek knowledge. They have a different goal; their goal is salvation from suffering. This is that which Gotama teaches, and nothing else."

"May you, O exalted one, not scorn me," said the young man. "I have not spoken to you like this to quarrel with you, to argue about words. You are truly right: opinions are insubstantial. But let me say this one more thing: I have not doubted in you for a single moment. I have not doubted for a single moment that you are Buddha who has reached the goal, the highest goal towards which so many thousands of Brahmins and sons of Brahmins are on their way. You have found salvation from death. It has come to you in the course of your own search, on your own path, through thoughts, through meditation, through realization, through enlightenment. It has not come to you by means of teachings! And—so are my thoughts, O exalted one—nobody will partake in salvation through teachings! You will not be able to convey and share with anyone, O venerable one, in words and through teachings what has happened to you in the hour of enlightenment! The teachings of the enlightened Buddha contain much. They teach many to live righteously and avoid evil. But there is one thing which these lucid and honorable teachings do not contain: they do not contain the mystery of what the exalted one alone among hundreds of thousands has experienced for himself. This is what I have thought and realized when I heard the teachings. This is why I am continuing my travels—not to seek other, better teachings, for I know there aren't any, but to depart from all teachings and all teachers and either to reach my goal on my own or to die. But I'll often think of this day, oh exalted one, and of this hour, when my eyes beheld a saint."

The Buddha's eyes quietly looked to the ground; quietly, in perfect equanimity his inscrutable face was smiling.

"May your thoughts," the venerable one spoke slowly, "not be in error! May you reach the goal! But tell me: Have you seen the multitude of my Samanas, my many brothers who have taken refuge in the teachings? And do you believe, O stranger, O Samana, do you believe that it would be better for them all to abandon the teachings and return into the life of the world and desires?"

"Such a thought is far from my mind," exclaimed Siddhartha. "Would that they all stay with the teachings, that they reach their goal! It is not my place to judge another person's life. Only for myself, for myself alone, must I pass judgment, choose, or reject. Salvation from the self is what we Samanas search for, O exalted one. If I were now one of your disciples, O honorable one, I fear that it may come to pass that my existence would only appear to be calm and redeemed, but in reality my inner being would live on and grow large because I had replaced my inner being with teachings, my duty to follow you, my love for you, and with the community of monks!"

With half of a smile, with an unwavering openness and kindness, Gotama looked into the stranger's eyes and bid him to leave with an almost imperceptible gesture.

"You are wise, O Samana." said the venerable one. "You know how to talk wisely, my friend. Be wary of too much wisdom!"

The Buddha turned away, and his glance and half-smile remained forever etched in Siddhartha's memory.

"I have never before seen a person glance and smile, sit and walk that way," he thought. "Truly, I want to be able to glance and smile, sit and walk that way, too: so free, so venerable, so concealed, so open, so child-like and mysterious. Truly, only a person who has succeeded in reaching the innermost part of his self would glance and walk this way. Truly, I also will seek to reach the innermost part of my self."

"I saw a person," Siddhartha thought, "a single one before whom I had to lower my glance. I do not want to lower my glance before any other, not before any other. No teachings will entice me any more, since this man's teachings have not enticed me."

"The Buddha has robbed me," thought Siddhartha, "he has robbed me, and he has given as a gift much more to me. He has robbed me of my friend, the one who had believed in me and now believes in him, who had been my shadow and is now Gotama's shadow. But he has given me Siddhartha, myself."

Awakening

WHEN SIDDHARTHA LEFT the grove where Buddha, the perfected one, stayed behind, and where Govinda stayed behind, he felt that in this grove his past life also stayed behind and separated from him. This sensation that filled him so completely was something that he pondered as he walked slowly along. He pondered deeply, like diving into deep water: he let himself sink down to the bottom of the sensation, down to the place where the causes lie. He did so because identifying causes, so it seemed to him, was the very essence of thinking, and by this act alone sensations turn into realizations and are not lost, but become entities and start to emit like rays of light what is inside of them.

Slowly walking along, Siddhartha pondered. He realized that he was no longer a youth, but had turned into a man. He realized that one thing had left him, as a snake left its old skin; one thing which had accompanied him throughout his youth and used to be a part of him no longer existed inside him: the desire to have teachers and to listen to teachings. He had also left the last teacher who had appeared on his path, even the highest and wisest teacher, the most holy one, the Buddha. He had left him, parted from him, and was not able to accept his teachings.

The thinker walked forward more slowly, asking himself: "But what is it that you wanted to learn from teachings and from teachers that they, who have taught you much, were still unable to impart to you?" And he found: "It was the self, the purpose and essence of which I sought to learn. It was the self from which I sought freedom and that I wanted to overcome. But I was not able to overcome it; I could only deceive it, flee from it, hide from it. Truly, no thing in this world has so occupied my thoughts as has my own self, the riddle of the fact I am alive, that I am distinct and separate from all others, that I am Siddhartha! And there is no thing in this world I know less about than about me, about Siddhartha!"

After ruminating over this while he was walking along, he stopped as these thoughts caught hold of him, and immediately another thought sprang forth from these, a new thought, namely: "The fact that I know nothing about myself, that Siddhartha has remained alien and unknown to me, stems from one cause, a single cause: I was afraid of myself, I was fleeing from myself! I searched Atman, I searched Brahman, I was willing to dissect my self and peel off all of its layers, to find the core of all peels in its unknown interior, the Atman, life, the divine part, the ultimate part. But I have lost myself in the process."

Siddhartha opened his eyes and looked around; a smile filled his face and a profound feeling of awakening from long dreams flowed through him from his head down to his toes. And it was not long before he walked again, this time walking quickly like a man who knows what he must do.

"Ah," he thought, taking a deep breath, "this time I won't allow Siddhartha to escape from me again! I no longer want to begin my thoughts and my life with Atman and with the suffering of the world. I no longer want to kill and dissect myself just to find a secret behind the ruins. Neither Yoga-Veda[†] shall teach me any more, nor Atharva-Veda, nor the ascetics, nor any kind of teachings. I want to learn from myself, want to be my student, want to get to know myself, the secret of Siddhartha."

He looked around, as if he were seeing the world for the first time. The world was beautiful and colorful; the world was strange and mysterious! Here was blue, here was yellow, here was green; the sky and the river flowed, the forest and the mountains were fixed in their places. All of it was beautiful, all of it was mysterious and magical, and in its midst he, Siddhartha, the awakening one, was on the path to himself. All of this—the yellow and blue, river and forest—entered Siddhartha for the first time through the eyes; it was no longer a spell of Mara,[†] no longer the veil of Maya,[†] no longer a pointless and coincidental diversity of mere appearances, despicable to the Brahmin of deep thoughts who scorns diversity and seeks unity. Blue was blue, river was river, and if the divine principle lay hidden within the blue and the river that lived within Siddhartha, so it was divinity's way and purpose for there to be here yellow, here blue, there sky, there forest, and here Siddhartha. The purpose and the essential properties were not somewhere behind the things; they were in them, in everything.

"How deaf and stupid I have been!" he thought, walking swiftly along. "When someone reads a text and wants to discover its meaning, he will not scorn the symbols and letters and call them deceptions, coincidence, and worthless shells, but he will read them, he will study and love them, letter by letter. But I, who wanted to read the book of the world and the book of my own being, I have, for the sake of a meaning I had assumed before I read, scorned the symbols and letters, I called the visible world a deception, called my eyes and my tongue coincidental and worthless forms without substance. No, this is over; I have awakened, I have indeed awakened and have not been born before this very day."

In thinking these thoughts, Siddhartha stopped once again, suddenly, as if a snake were lying in front of him on the path.

Because suddenly, this had also become clear to him: he, who was indeed like someone who had just woken up or like a new-born baby, had to start his life anew from the very beginning. When he left the grove of Jetavana this very morning, the grove of that exalted one, already awakening and already on the path towards himself, he had taken for granted and considered it only natural that he, after years as an ascetic, would return to his home and his father. But it was only in this moment when he stopped as if a snake were lying on his path that he came to this realization: "But I am no longer the person I was, I am no longer an ascetic, I am no longer a priest, I am no longer a Brahmin. Whatever would I do at my father's place, at home? Study? Make offerings? Practice meditation? But all this is over, none of this is now on my path."

Motionless, Siddhartha remained standing there, and for the span of one moment and breath, his heart felt cold. He felt a chill in his chest, just as a small animal, such as a bird or a rabbit, would when seeing how alone he was. For many years, he had been without home and had felt nothing. Now, he felt it. Still, even in the deepest meditation, he had been his father's son, had been a Brahmin, a cleric of a high caste. Now, he was nothing but Siddhartha, the awoken one; nothing else was left. He inhaled deeply, and for a moment, he felt cold, and he shivered. There was no one who was alone as he was. There was no nobleman who did not belong among the noblemen, no worker that did not belong with the workers and found refuge among them, shared their life, spoke their language. There was no Brahmin who would not be regarded as a Brahmin and live with them, no ascetic who would not find shelter in the Samana caste, and even the most forlorn hermit in the forest was not alone, he was also surrounded by a place to which he belonged. He also belonged to a caste where he was at home. Govinda had become a monk, and the thousand monks who were his brothers wore the same robe as he did, believed in his faith, spoke his language. But where did Siddhartha belong? With whom would he share his life? Whose language would he speak?

Out of this moment when the world melted away all around him, when he stood alone like a star in the sky, out of this moment of cold and despair, Siddhartha emerged, more himself than before, firmer in his resolve. He sensed that this had been the last tremor of the awakening, the final pangs of this birth. And it was not long until he walked again in long strides, started to proceed swiftly and impatiently, as he headed no longer for home, no longer to his father, no longer backwards.

SECOND PART

SIDDHARTHA

Kamala

SIDDHARTHA LEARNED something new on every step of his path,
for the world was transformed, and his heart was enchanted. He saw
the sun rising over the forest-covered mountains and setting over the
distant palm beaches. At night, he saw the stars in the sky in their fixed
positions and the crescent of the moon floating like a boat in the deep
blue. He saw trees, stars, animals, clouds, rainbows, rocks, herbs, flowers,
stream and river, the glistening dew in the bushes in the morning, distant
high mountains pale and blue, singing birds and the bees, wind wafting
like silver through the rice fields. All of these thousands of colorful things
had always been there; the sun and the moon had always shone, rivers had
always roared and bees had always buzzed, but in former times all of this
had been nothing more to Siddhartha than a fleeting, deceptive veil before
his eyes. He had looked upon these with mistrust, as if their destiny was
to be penetrated and destroyed by thought, since material things were not
essential to existence, the essence of which lay beyond, on the other side
of what was visible. But now, his liberated eyes stayed on this side; he saw
and became aware of that which was visible and sought to be at home in
this world. He did not search for true essence and did not aim at a world
beyond. It was beautiful and wonderful to go through the world in this
childlike way. The moon and the stars were beautiful, as were the stream
and the riverbanks, the forest and the rocks, the goat and the gold beetle,
the flower and the butterfly. It was lovely and beautiful to walk through
the world like this, childlike and fully awake, open to what is near and
without mistrust. The sun shone differently upon the head, the shade of

the forest cooled him differently, the stream and the cistern were different, the pumpkin and the banana tasted different. The days were short, the nights also short; every hour sped swiftly away like a sail on the sea, and under the sail was a ship full of treasures and joy. Siddhartha saw a troop of monkeys moving through the high canopy of the forest in the branches and heard their savage, greedy song. Siddhartha saw a male sheep following a female one and mating with her. In a lake of reeds, he saw the pike hungrily hunting its dinner; he saw young fish propelling themselves away from it in fear, wiggling and sparkling, jumping in droves out of the water. The scent of strength and passion came forcefully out of the swift eddies of the water which were stirred up by the pike, who hunted endlessly.

All of this had always existed, and he had not seen it; he had not been with it. Now he was with it, he was part of it. Light and shadow ran through his eyes, and the stars and moon ran through his heart.

On the way, Siddhartha also recollected everything he had experienced in the Garden of Jetavana: the teaching he had heard there, the divine Buddha, the farewell from Govinda, his conversation with the exalted one. He remembered again the words that he had spoken to the exalted one, every word, and with astonishment he became aware of the fact that there he had said things which he had not really known. What he had said to Gotama—that is, that the Buddha's treasure and secret was not the teachings, but the ineffable and non-transferable thing that he had experienced in the hour of his enlightenment—it was this very thing which he had now gone to experience and now began to experience. He now had to experience his self. It is true that he had already known for a long time that his self was Atman, in its essence bearing the same eternal characteristics as Brahman. But he had never really found this self because he had wanted to capture it in the snare of thought. The body was certainly not the self, and the game of the senses wasn't, and in the same way neither thoughts, nor the rational mind, nor learned wisdom, nor the learned ability to draw conclusions and to develop new thoughts from prior ones was the self. No, this world of thought was also still on this side, and it was pointless to kill the coincidental self of the senses, if the coincidental self of thoughts and learned knowledge was fattened thereby. Both, the thoughts as well as the senses, were pretty things, and the ultimate meaning was hidden behind both of them. Both had to be listened to, both had to be played with, both should be neither scorned nor overestimated; both secret voices of the innermost truth had to be clearly perceived. He wanted to strive for nothing but what the voice commanded him to strive for, dwell on nothing but what the voice would have him do. Why had Gotama, in the hour of all hours, seated himself down under the fig tree where the enlightenment struck him? He had heard a voice, a voice in his own heart, which had commanded him to seek rest under this tree, and he had neither preferred self-castigation, offerings, ablutions, nor prayer, neither food nor drink, neither sleep nor dream; he had obeyed the voice. To be obedient like this (not to an external command, only to the voice), to be ready like this, was both good and necessary. Nothing else was necessary.

In the night when he slept in the straw hut of a ferryman by the river, Siddhartha had a dream: Govinda was standing in front of him, dressed in the yellow robe of an ascetic. Govinda looked sad, and in a sad voice he asked: "Why have you forsaken me?" At this, Siddhartha embraced Govinda, wrapped his arms around him, and as he was pulling Govinda close to his chest and kissed him, it was not Govinda any more, but a female, and out of the female gown poured a spring from a full breast, at which Siddhartha lay and drank, and strong and sweet did the milk from this breast taste. It tasted of woman and man, of sun and forest, of animal and flower, of every fruit, of every desire. It made him drunk and unconscious.—When Siddhartha woke up, the pale river shimmered through the door of the hut, and in the forest, a dark call of an owl resounded deeply and pleasantly.

When the day began, Siddhartha asked his host, the ferryman, to get him across the river. The ferryman got him across the river on his bamboo raft while the wide water had a reddish sheen in the morning light.

"This is a beautiful river," he said to his companion.

"Yes," said the ferryman, "a very beautiful river; I love it more than anything. Often I have listened to it, often I have looked into its eyes, and always I have learned from it. One can learn much from a river."

"I thank you, my benefactor," spoke Siddhartha, disembarking on the other side of the river. "I have no gift I could give you for your hospitality, good sir, and also no payment for your work. I am a man without a home, a son of a Brahmin and a Samana."

"I did see it," spoke the ferryman, "and I expected no payment from you and no gift in exchange for hospitality. You will give me the gift another time."

"Do you think so?" asked Siddhartha amusedly.

"Surely. This too, I have learned from the river: everything comes again! You too, Samana, will come again. Now farewell! Let your friendship be my reward. May you think of me when you make offerings to the gods."

Smiling, they parted. Smiling, Siddhartha was happy about the friendship and the kindness of the ferryman. "He is like Govinda," he thought with a smile, "all I meet on my path are like Govinda. All are thankful, though they are the ones who would have a right to receive thanks. They are all submissive, they all want to be friends, happily obeying and not thinking much. People are all like children."

Around noon, he passed through a village. In front of the mud cottages, children were rolling about in the street, playing with pumpkin-seeds and sea-shells, screaming and wrestling. The children all fled timidly from the unknown Samana. In the end of the village, the path led through a stream, and by the side of the stream, a young woman was kneeling and washing clothes. When Siddhartha greeted her, she lifted her head and looked up at him with a smile; he saw the white in her eyes glistening. He called out a blessing to her, as is customary among travelers, and asked how far he still had to go to reach the large city. Then she got up and came to him, her moist lips shimmering beautifully in her young face. She exchanged humorous banter with him, asked whether he had eaten already, and whether it was true that the Samanas slept alone in the forest at night and were not allowed to have any women with them. While talking, she put her left foot on his right one and made a movement as a woman does when they want to initiate sexual pleasure with a man of the kind which the textbooks call "climbing a tree." Siddhartha felt his blood heating up, and since in this moment he had to think of his dream again, he bend slightly down to the woman and kissed with his lips the brown nipple of her breast. Looking up, he saw her face smiling full of desire; her eyes, with contracted pupils, begged with longing.

Siddhartha also felt desire and felt the source of his sexuality stirring; but since he had never touched a woman before, he hesitated for a moment; his hands were already prepared to reach out for her. And in this moment he heard, shuddering with awe, the voice of his innermost self, and this voice said No. Then, all charms disappeared from the young woman's smiling face; he no longer saw anything else but the sweaty glance of a female animal in heat. Politely, he petted her cheek, turned away from her and, with light steps, he vanished away from the disappointed woman into the bamboo wood.

On this day, he reached the large city before the evening. He was happy, for he felt the need to be among people. He had lived in the forests for quite some time, and the straw hut of the ferryman, in which he had slept that night, had been the first roof in a long while that had been over his head.

Before the city, in a beautifully fenced grove, the traveler came across a small group of servants, both male and female, carrying baskets. In their midst, carried by four servants in an ornamental sedan-chair, sat a woman on red pillows under a colorful canopy—their mistress. Siddhartha stopped at the entrance to the pleasure-garden and watched the parade;

he saw the servants, the maids, the baskets, the sedan-chair and the lady within it. Under black hair, which towered high on her head, he saw a very fair, very delicate, and very smart face; a bright red mouth, like a freshly cracked fig, eyebrows which were well tended and painted in a high arch, and intelligent, watchful, dark eyes adorned this face. She had a clear, tall neck rising from a gold and green garment, still, fair hands that were long and thin, and wide golden bracelets over her wrists.

Siddhartha saw how beautiful she was, and his heart rejoiced. He bowed deeply when the sedan-chair came closer, and, straightening up again, he looked at the fair, charming face, read for a moment the intelligent eyes with the high arches above it, breathed in a slight fragrance which he did not know. With a smile, the beautiful women nodded for a moment and disappeared into the grove, and then the servants went as well.

Thus I am entering this city, Siddhartha thought, with a charming omen. He instantly felt drawn into the grove, but he thought about it, and only now became aware of how the servants and maids had looked at him at the entrance, with scorn, with mistrust, with rejection.

I am still a Samana, he thought, I am still an ascetic and beggar. I must not remain like this; I will not be able to enter the grove like this. And he laughed.

He asked the next person who came along his way about the grove and the name of the woman, and he was told that this was the grove of Kamala, the famous courtesan, and that in addition to the grove, she owned a house in the city.

He then entered the city. He now had a goal.

He allowed the city to suck him in as he pursued his goal. He drifted through the flow of the streets, stood still in the squares, rested on the the stone stairs by the river. When evening came, he became friends with a barber's assistant whom he had seen working in the shade of a building's arch, whom he found again praying in a temple of Vishnu,[†] and whom he told stories of Vishnu and the Lakshmi.[†] He slept among the boats by the river this night, and early in the morning, before the first customers came into his shop, he had the barber's assistant shave his beard and cut his hair, comb his hair and anoint it with fine oil. Then he went to bathe in the river.

When the beautiful Kamala approached her grove in her sedan-chair late in the afternoon, Siddhartha was standing at the entrance. He made a bow and received the courtesan's greeting. He motioned to the servant who walked at the very end of her train and asked him to inform his mistress that a young Brahmin would like to speak with her. After a while, the servant returned, gesturing for the guest to follow him. Without a word the servant conducted Siddhartha into a pavilion, where Kamala was lying on a couch, and the servant left him alone with her.

"Weren't you standing out there just yesterday, greeting me?" asked Kamala.

"It's true that I've seen you and greeted you only yesterday."

"But didn't you wear a beard yesterday, and have long hair with dust in it?"

"You have observed well; you have seen everything. You have seen Siddhartha, the son of a Brahmin, who has left his home to become a Samana, and who has been a Samana for three years. But I have now left that path and come into this city, and, even before I had entered the city, the first one I met was you. I say this: I have come to you, O Kamala! You are the first woman whom Siddhartha addresses without downcast eyes. I never again want to turn my eyes toward the ground when I encounter a beautiful woman."

Kamala smiled and played with her fan of peacock feathers. She asked: "Was it only to tell me this that Siddhartha has come to me?"

"To tell you this and to thank you for being so beautiful. And, if it doesn't displease you, Kamala, I would like to ask you to be my friend and teacher, for I know nothing yet of that art which you have mastered in the highest degree."

At this, Kamala laughed aloud.

"Never before this has happened to me, my friend, that a Samana from the forest came to me and wanted to learn from me! Never before this has happened to me, that a Samana came to me with long hair and an old, torn loincloth! Many young men come to me, and among them are also sons of Brahmins, but they come in beautiful clothes and fine shoes, with perfume in their hair and money in their pouches. This, oh Samana, is what the young men who come to me are like."

Said Siddhartha: "I am already starting to learn from you. I was already learning even yesterday. I have already taken off my beard, combed my hair, and have oil in my hair. There is little that I still lack, O excellent one: fine clothes, fine shoes, and money in my pouch. You should know that Siddhartha has set harder goals for himself than such trifles, and he has reached them. How then should I not reach the goal which I have set for myself yesterday: to be your friend and to learn the joys of love from you? You'll see that I'll learn quickly, Kamala; I have already learned harder things than that which you should teach me. And so: you aren't satisfied with Siddhartha as he is, with oil in his hair, but without clothes, shoes, or money?"

Laughing, Kamala exclaimed: "No, precious, he doesn't satisfy me yet. Clothes are what he must have, pretty clothes, and shoes, pretty shoes, and lots of money in his pouch, and gifts for Kamala. Do you know it now, Samana from the forest? Did you mark my words?"

"Yes, I have marked your words," Siddhartha exclaimed. "How should I not mark words that come from such a mouth! Your mouth is like a freshly cracked fig, Kamala. My mouth is red and fresh as well; it will be a suitable match for yours, you'll see. But tell me, beautiful Kamala, do you not have any fear of the Samana from the forest who has come here to learn love?"

"Why should I fear a Samana, a stupid Samana from the forest, who is coming from the jackals and doesn't even know yet what women are?"

"Oh, he's strong, the Samana, and he fears nothing. He could force you, beautiful girl. He could abduct you. He could hurt you."

"No, Samana, I am not afraid of this. Did any Samana or Brahmin ever fear that someone might come and grab him and steal his learning, and his religious devotion, and his depth of thought? No, for they are his very own, and he would only give away from those whatever he is willing to give and to whomever he is willing to give. It is like this, precisely like this, with Kamala and with the pleasures of love. Kamala's mouth is beautiful and red, but just try to kiss it against Kamala's will, and you will not obtain a single drop of sweetness from that which knows how to give so many sweet things! You are learning easily, Siddhartha, and you should also learn this: love can be obtained by begging, buying, receiving it as a gift, or finding it in the street, but it cannot be stolen. In this, you have come up with the wrong plan. No, it would be a pity if a handsome young man like you would attack it in such a wrong manner."

Siddhartha bowed with a smile. "It would be a pity, Kamala, you are right! It would be such a great pity. No, I shall not lose a single drop of sweetness from your mouth, nor you from mine! So it is settled: Siddhartha will return, once he has what he still lacks: clothes, shoes, money. But speak, lovely Kamala, couldn't you still give me one small piece of advice?"

"A piece of advice? Why not? Who wouldn't want to give advice to a poor, ignorant Samana coming from the jackals of the forest?"

"Dear Kamala, then advise me about where I should go to find these three things most readily?"

"Friend, many would like to know this. You must do what you've learned and ask for money, clothes, and shoes in return. There is no other way for a poor man to obtain money. What might you be able to do?"

"I can think. I can wait. I can fast."

"Nothing else?"

"Nothing. No, on the contrary, I can also write poetry. Would you like to give me a kiss for a poem?"

"I will do that if your poem pleases me. What is it called, then?"

Siddhartha spoke, after he had thought about it for a moment, these verses:

Into her shady grove stepped the beautiful Kamala,
At the grove's entrance stood the brown Samana.
Spotting the lotus's blossom, deeply
Bowed that man, and, smiling, Kamala thanked him.
More lovely, thought the young man, than offerings for gods,
More lovely are offerings to beautiful Kamala.

Kamala clapped her hands loudly so that the golden bracelets jingled.

"Your verses are beautiful, oh brown Samana, and I'm truly losing nothing when I'm giving you a kiss for them."

She beckoned him with her eyes; he tilted his head so that his face touched hers and placed his mouth on that mouth which was like a freshly cracked fig. For a long time, Kamala kissed him, and with deep astonishment Siddhartha felt how she taught him, how wise she was, how she controlled him, rejected him, lured him, and how after this first one there was a long, well-ordered, well-practiced sequence of kisses, every one different from the others, that he was still to receive. Breathing deeply, he remained standing where he was, and was in this moment astonished like a child about the cornucopia of knowledge and things worth learning, which were revealed before his eyes.

"Very beautiful are your verses," exclaimed Kamala, "if I were rich, I would give you pieces of gold for them. But it will be difficult for you to earn as much money as you need with verses. You need a lot of money, if you want to be Kamala's friend."

"The way you're able to kiss, Kamala!" stammered Siddhartha.

"Yes, this I am able to do, therefore I do not lack clothes, shoes, bracelets, and all beautiful things. But what will become of you? Aren't you able to do anything else but think, fast, and make poetry?"

"I also know the sacrificial songs," said Siddhartha, "but I do not want to sing them any more. I also know magic spells, but I do not want to speak them any more. I have read the scriptures—"

"Stop," Kamala interrupted him. "You're able to read? And write?"

"Certainly, I can do this. Many people can do this."

"Most people can't. I can't do it, either. It is very good that you're able to read and write, very good. You will also find use for those magic spells."

In this moment, a maid came running in and whispered a message into her mistress's ear.

"I have a visitor," exclaimed Kamala. "Hurry and get yourself away, Siddhartha. Nobody may see you in here; remember this! Tomorrow, I'll see you again."

But to the maid she gave the order to give the pious Brahmin white garments. Without fully understanding what was happening to him, Siddhartha found himself being dragged away by the maid, brought into a garden-house by avoiding the direct path, being given upper garments as a gift, led into the bushes, and urgently admonished to get himself out of the grove as soon as possible without being seen.

Content, he did as he had been told. Being accustomed to the forest, he managed to get out of the grove and over the hedge without making a sound. Content, he returned to the city, carrying the rolled-up garments under his arm. At the inn where travelers stay, he positioned himself by the door, asking without words for food. Without a word he accepted a piece of rice-cake. Perhaps as soon as tomorrow, he thought, I will ask no one for food any more.

Suddenly, pride flared up in him. He was no Samana any more; it was no longer becoming for him to beg. He gave the rice cake to a dog and remained without food.

"The life which people lead here in this world is easy," thought Siddhartha. "It presents no difficulties. Everything was difficult, toilsome, and ultimately hopeless, when I was still a Samana. Now, everything is easy, easy like that lesson in kissing which Kamala is giving me. I need clothes and money, nothing else; this is a small, near goal, and nobody would lose sleep over it."

He had already discovered Kamala's house in the city long before, and he showed up there the following day.

"Things are working out well," she called out to him. "They are expecting you at Kamaswami's; he is the richest merchant of the city. If you please him, he'll accept you into his service. Be shrewd, brown Samana. I told him about you through others. Be polite towards him; he is very powerful. But don't be too modest! I don't want you to become his servant. You shall become his equal, or else I won't be satisfied with you. Kamaswami is starting to get old and lazy. If he likes you, he'll entrust you with a lot."

Siddhartha thanked her and laughed, and when she found out that he had not eaten anything yesterday or today, she sent for bread and fruits and treated him to them.

"You've been lucky," she said when they parted, "I'm opening one door after another for you. How does that happen? Do you have a spell?"

Siddhartha said: "Yesterday, I told you I knew how to think, to wait, and to fast. You, however, thought this was of no use. Yet it is useful for many things, Kamala; you'll see. You'll see that the stupid Samanas learn and accomplish many beautiful things in the forest that you all cannot. The day before yesterday, I was still a shaggy beggar; as soon as yesterday I kissed Kamala, and soon I'll be a merchant and have money and all those things that you value."

"Well yes," she admitted. "But where would you be without me? What would you be, if Kamala weren't helping you?"

"Dear Kamala," said Siddhartha he straightened up to his full height, "when I came to you into your grove, I took the first step. It was my resolution to learn love from this most beautiful woman. From the moment when I had made this resolution, I also knew that I would carry it out. I knew that you would help me, at your first glance at the entrance of the grove I already knew it."

"But what if I hadn't been willing?"

"You were willing. Look, Kamala: When you throw a rock into the water, it hurries on the fastest course to the bottom of the water. This is how it is when Siddhartha has a goal, a resolution. Siddhartha does nothing; he waits, he thinks, he fasts, but he passes through the things of the world like a rock through water, without doing anything, without stirring. He is drawn; he lets himself fall. His goal attracts him, because he doesn't let anything enter his soul which might oppose the goal. This is what Siddhartha has learned among the Samanas. This is what foolish people call magic and what they think is brought about by means of the demons. Nothing is caused by demons; there are no demons. Everyone can perform magic; everyone can reach his goals, if he is able to think, to wait, and to fast."

Kamala listened to him. She loved his voice; she loved the look from his eyes.

"Perhaps it is so," she said quietly, "as you say, friend. But perhaps it is also like this: that Siddhartha is a handsome man, that his glance pleases women, and that therefore good fortune is coming towards him."

Siddhartha took his leave with a kiss. "May it be so, my teacher; may my glance always please you, may good fortune always come to me from your direction!"

With the Childlike People

S IDDHARTHA WENT TO Kamaswami the merchant; he was directed
to an opulent house. Servants led him between precious carpets into
a chamber where he awaited the master of the house.

Kamaswami entered, a swiftly, smoothly moving man with very gray
hair, very intelligent, cautious eyes, and a greedy mouth. The host and the
guest greeted one another politely.

"I have been told," the merchant began, "that you were a Brahmin, a
learned man, but that you seek to be in the service of a merchant. Did you
become destitute, Brahmin, that you seek to enter service?"

"No," said Siddhartha, "I have not become destitute and have never
been destitute. You should know that I'm coming from the Samanas, with
whom I have lived for a long time."

"If you're coming from the Samanas, how could you be anything but
destitute? Aren't the Samanas entirely without possessions?"

"I am without possessions," said Siddhartha, "if this is what you mean.
Of course I am without possessions. But I am so voluntarily, and therefore
I am not destitute."

"How will you gain a living, being without possessions?"

"I haven't thought of this yet, sir. For more than three years, I have
been without possessions, and have never thought about what I should
live on."

"So you've lived off the possessions of others."

"I suppose that is so. Even a merchant lives off what other
people own."

"Well said. But he wouldn't take anything from another person for nothing; he would give his merchandise in return."

"So it seems to be indeed. Everyone takes, everyone gives, such is life."

"But allow me to ask: being without possessions, what would you like to give?"

"Everyone gives what he has. The warrior gives strength, the merchant gives merchandise, the teacher lessons, the farmer rice, the fisherman fish."

"Yes indeed. And what is it now that you have to give? What is it that you've learned, what are you able to do?"

"I can think. I can wait. I can fast."

"That's everything?"

"I believe that's everything!"

"And what's the use of that? For example, the fasting—what is it good for?"

"It is very good, sir. When a person has nothing to eat, fasting is the smartest thing he could do. If, for example, Siddhartha hadn't learned to fast, he would have to accept any kind of service before this day is up, whether with you or wherever, because hunger would force him to do so. But as it stands, Siddhartha can wait calmly. He knows no impatience, he knows no emergency. He can allow hunger to besiege him for a long time and can laugh about it. This, sir, is what fasting is good for."

"You're right, Samana. Wait for a moment."

Kamaswami left the room and returned with a scroll, which he handed to his guest while asking: "Can you read this?"

Siddhartha looked at the scroll, on which a sales contract had been written down, and began to read out its contents.

"Excellent," said Kamaswami. "And would you write something for me on this piece of paper?"

He handed him a piece of paper and a pen, and Siddhartha wrote and returned the paper.

Kamaswami read: "Writing is good, but thinking is better. Intelligence is good, but patience is better."

"You understand writing excellently," the merchant praised him. "We will still have to discuss certain things with one another. For today, I'm asking you to be my guest and to live in this house."

Siddhartha thanked him and accepted, and lived in the merchant's house from then on. Clothes were brought to him, and shoes, and every day a servant prepared a bath for him. Twice a day, a plentiful meal was served, but Siddhartha only ate once a day, and he neither ate meat nor drank wine. Kamaswami told him about his trade, showed him the merchandise and storage-rooms, showed him calculations. Siddhartha came to know many new things; he heard much and spoke little. And, thinking of Kamala's words, he was never subservient to the merchant, forcing him to treat him as an equal—yes, even more than an equal. Kamaswami conducted his business with care and often with passion, but Siddhartha looked upon all of this as if it were a game, the rules of which he tried hard to learn precisely, but the subject of which did not touch his heart.

He was not in Kamaswami's house long before he began to take part in his landlord's business. Daily, at the very hour appointed by her, he visited beautiful Kamala while wearing handsome clothes and fine shoes; he soon brought her gifts as well. He learned much from her red, shrewd mouth. He learned much from her tender, supple hand. He was, regarding love, still a boy and had a tendency to plunge blindly and insatiably into lust like into a bottomless pit; she taught him, starting with the basics, about that school of thought which teaches that pleasure cannot be taken without giving pleasure, and that every gesture, every caress, every touch, every look, every area of the body, however small it was, had a secret which would bring happiness to those who know about it and unleash it. She taught him that lovers must not part from one another after celebrating love without admiring one another, without being just as defeated as they are victorious, so that neither one started feeling fed up or bored and get that wicked feeling of having abused or having been abused. He spent wonderful hours with the beautiful and intelligent artist, became her student, her lover, her friend. The worth and purpose of his present life was here with Kamala, not with the business of Kamaswami.

The merchant transferred the duty of writing important letters and contracts on to Siddhartha and became accustomed to discussing all important affairs with him. He soon saw that Siddhartha knew little about rice and wool, shipping and trade, but that he acted in a fortunate manner, and that Siddhartha surpassed him, the merchant, in calmness and equanimity, in the art of listening and deeply understanding previously unknown people. "This Brahmin," he said to a friend, "is no proper merchant and will never be one, there is never any passion in his soul when he conducts our business. But he has that mysterious quality of those people to whom success comes all by itself, perhaps as a result of a good star during his birth, magic, or something he has learned among Samanas. He always seems to be merely playing with business affairs; they never fully become a part of him and they never rule over him. He is never afraid of failure; he is never upset by a loss."

The friend advised the merchant: "Give him from the business he conducts for you a third of the profits, but let him also be liable for the same amount of the losses, when there is a loss. Then, he'll become more zealous."

Kamaswami followed the advice. But Siddhartha cared little about this. When he made a profit, he accepted it with equanimity; when he made losses, he laughed and said: "Well, look at this; this one turned out badly!"

It seemed indeed, as if he did not care about the business. At one time, he traveled to a village to buy a large harvest of rice there. But when he got there, the rice had already been sold to another merchant. Nevertheless, Siddhartha stayed for several days in that village, treated the farmers to a drink, gave copper-coins to their children, joined in the celebration of a wedding, and returned extremely satisfied from his trip. Kamaswami held against him that he had not turned back right away, that he had wasted time and money. Siddhartha answered: "Stop scolding, dear friend! Nothing was ever achieved by scolding. If a loss has occurred, let me bear that loss. I am very satisfied with this trip. I have gotten to know myriad people. A Brahmin has become my friend, children have sat on my knees, farmers have shown me their fields, nobody knew that I was a merchant."

"That's all very nice," exclaimed Kamaswami indignantly, "but on the contrary, you are in fact a merchant, I should think! Or might you have only traveled for your amusement?"

"Surely," Siddhartha laughed, "surely I have traveled for my amusement. For what else? I have gotten to know people and places, I have received kindness and trust, I have found friendship. Look, my good man, if I had been Kamaswami, I would have traveled back, annoyed and in a hurry, as soon as I had seen that my purchase had been rendered impossible. Time and money would indeed have been lost. But as it stands, I've had a few good days, I've learned and had joy, and I've neither harmed myself nor others through annoyance and hastiness. And if I ever return there again, perhaps to buy an upcoming harvest, or for whatever purpose it might be, friendly people will receive me in a friendly and happy manner, and I will praise myself for not showing any hurry and displeasure at that time. So, leave it as it is, my friend, and don't harm yourself by scolding! If the day comes when you say "this Siddhartha is harming me," then speak a word and Siddhartha will go on his own path. But until then, let's be satisfied with one another."

The merchant's attempts to convince Siddhartha that he should eat his bread were also futile. Siddhartha ate his own bread, or rather they both ate other people's bread, all people's bread. Siddhartha never listened to Kamaswami's worries, and Kamaswami had many worries. Whether there was a business deal going on which was in danger of failing, or whether a shipment of merchandise seemed to have been lost or a debtor seemed to be unable to pay, Kamaswami could never convince his partner that it would be useful to utter a few words of worry or anger, to have wrinkles on the forehead, to sleep restlessly. When, one day, Kamaswami told Siddhartha that he had learned everything he knew from him, Siddhartha replied: "Quit pulling my leg with these games! What I've learned from you is how much a basket of fish costs and how interests may be charged on money loans. These are your areas of expertise. I haven't learned to think from you, my dear Kamaswami; you ought to be the one seeking to learn from me."

Indeed, his heart was not in the trade. The business was good enough to provide him with the money for Kamala, and it earned him much more than he needed. Apart from this, Siddhartha's interest and curiosity were concerned only with the people whose businesses, crafts, worries, pleasures, and acts of foolishness used to be as alien and distant to him as the moon. However easily he succeeded in talking to all of them, in living with all of them, in learning from all of them, he was still aware that there was something that separated him from them: this was the fact that he was a Samana. He saw mankind going through life like a child or an animal that he both loved and despised at the same time. He saw them toiling, suffering, and becoming gray-haired for the sake of things which seemed to him entirely unworthy of this price. He saw them scolding and insulting each other for money, for small pleasures, or for some small encomium; he saw them complain about pain at which a Samana would only smile, and suffering because of deprivations which a Samana would not feel.

He was open to everything these people brought to him. The merchant who offered him linen for sale was welcome, the debtor who sought another loan was welcome, and also welcome was the beggar who for one hour told Siddhartha the story of poverty, although the beggar was not half as poor as any Samana. He did not treat the rich foreign merchant any different from the servant who shaved him and the street-vendor whom he let cheat him out of some small change when buying bananas. When Kamaswami came to him, complaining about his worries or reproaching him concerning business, he listened curiously and happily. He was puzzled by him, tried to understand him, let him win some arguments (at least, as many as it seemed he had to), and turned away from him towards the next person who would ask for him. And there were many who came to him to do business with him, to cheat him, to draw some secret out of him, to appeal to his sympathy, or to get his advice. He gave advice, pity, and gifts; he let them cheat him a little, and this entire game and the passion with which all people played this game occupied his thoughts just as much as the gods and Brahmins used to occupy them.

At times he felt, deep in his chest, a quiet, dying voice which admonished him with whispers, lamented softly; he hardly perceived it. And then, for an hour, he became aware of the strange life he was leading. He perceived himself doing lots of things which were only a game; he saw that, although happy and joyous at times, that real life was passing him by without touching him. As a ball-player plays with his balls, he played with his business-deals and with the people around him. He watched them and found amusement in them, but with his heart and the source of his being, he was not present with them. The source ran somewhere far away from him, ran and ran invisibly; it had nothing to do with his life any more. And at several times he suddenly became alarmed on account of such thoughts and wanted to be gifted with the ability to participate, with passion and with all his heart, in all of the childish and naïve occupations of the daytime. He really wanted to live, to act, and to enjoy instead of just standing by as a spectator. But again and again, he came back to the beautiful Kamala, learned the art of love, practiced the cult of lust, in which more than in anything else giving and taking become one, chatted with her, learned from her, gave her advice, and received advice. She understood him better than Govinda used to understand him; she was more similar to him.

Once he said to her: "You are like me, you are different from most people. You are Kamala, nothing else, and inside of you, there is a peace and refuge to which you can go at every hour of the day and be at home inside yourself, as I can also do. Few people have this, and yet everyone could have it."

"Not all people are clever," said Kamala.

"No," said Siddhartha, "that's not the reason why. Kamaswami is just as clever as I am, and yet he has no refuge in himself. Others who, in their minds, are small children with respect to their mind have it. Most people, Kamala, are like a falling leaf that is blown and is turning around through the air, wavering and tumbling to the ground. But others, a few, are like stars: they go on a fixed course, no wind reaches them, and in themselves they have their law and their direction. Among all the wise men and Samanas, of which I have known many, there was one of this type, a perfected one; I'll never be able to forget him. It is that Gotama, the exalted one, who is spreading those teachings. Thousands of followers are listening to his teachings every day, follow his instructions every hour, but they are all falling leaves and don't have in themselves the lesson or a law."

Kamala looked at him with a smile. "You're talking about him again," she said, "You're having a Samana's thoughts again."

Siddhartha said nothing, and they played the game of love, one of the thirty or forty different games Kamala knew. Her body was flexible like that of a jaguar and like the bow of a hunter; he who had learned from her how to make love was knowledgeable of many forms of desire, many secrets. She played with Siddhartha for a long time; she enticed him, rejected him, compelled him, embraced him. She enjoyed his masterful skills until he, defeated and exhausted, rested by her side.

The courtesan bent over him, took a long look at his face and at his eyes, which had grown tired.

"You are the best lover," she said thoughtfully, "I ever saw. You're stronger than others, more supple, more willing. You've learned my art well, Siddhartha. At some time, when I'm older, I want to bear your child. And even so, dear one, you've remained a Samana. You still don't love me; you love nobody. Isn't that so?"

"It might very well be so," Siddhartha said tiredly. "I am like you. You also do not love—how else could you practice love as a craft? Perhaps people of our kind can't love. The childlike people can; that's their secret."

Samsara†

SIDDHARTHA HAD LIVED the life of the world and of desire for a long time, though without being a part of it. His senses, which he had killed off in the heat of his years as a Samana, had awakened again. He had tasted riches, lust, and power; nevertheless he had still remained a Samana in his heart for a long time. Kamala, being clever, had quite astutely realized this. It was still the art of thinking, of waiting, and of fasting which guided his life. The people of the world, the childlike people, had still remained as strange to him as he was to them.

Years passed by; Siddhartha hardly felt them fading away while he was surrounded by the good life. He had become rich, and for quite a while he possessed a house of his own, his own servants, and a garden by the river near the city. The people liked him and they came to him whenever they needed money or advice, but there was nobody close to him except Kamala.

That high, bright state of being awake, which he had experienced that one time at the height of his youth in those days after Gotama's sermon, after he had separated from Govinda—that tense expectation, that proud state of standing alone without lessons and without teachers, that supple willingness to listen to the divine voice in his own heart—had slowly become a fleeting memory. The holy source, which used to be near and to murmur within himself, now murmured from afar. Nevertheless, many things that he had learned from the Samanas, from Gotama, or from his father the Brahmin had remained within him for a long time after-wards: moderate living, the joys of thinking, hours of meditation, secret knowledge of the self and of his eternal entity, which is neither body nor consciousness. He had retained many portions of this, but one part after another had been stifled and now gathered dust. Just as a potter's wheel, once it has been set in motion, will keep on turning for a long time and only slowly lose its vigor and come to a stop, Siddhartha's soul had kept on turning the wheel of asceticism, of thinking, and of discernment for a long time. It was still turning, but it turned slowly and hesitantly and was almost at a standstill. Gradually, like humidity entering the dying stem of a tree, filling it slowly and making it rot, the world and sloth had entered Siddhartha's soul. It gradually filled his soul, made it heavy and tired, and put it to sleep. On the other hand, his senses had become alive; they had learned and experienced a great deal.

Siddhartha had learned how to conduct trade and to use his power over people. He learned to enjoy himself with a woman, how to wear beautiful clothes, give orders to servants, and bathe in perfumed waters. He had learned how to eat food that was tenderly and carefully prepared —even fish, meat, poultry, spices, and sweets. He learned to drink wine, which causes laziness and forgetfulness. He had learned how to play dice and chess, how to watch dancing girls, how to sleep on a soft bed, and how to be carried about in a sedan-chair. However, he still felt different from and superior to the others; he always watched them with a certain amount of ridicule, with mocking disdain, and the same contempt that a Samana constantly feels for the people of the world. When Kamaswami felt ill, when he was annoyed, insulted, or vexed in his mercantile concerns, Siddhartha always looked on with mockery. As slowly and imperceptibly as the harvest and rainy seasons pass by, his mockery had become more tired and his superiority more subdued. Amidst his accumulating wealth, Siddhartha had gradually assumed something of the childlike people's ways for his own—something of their childlikeness and fearfulness. Even so, he envied them all the more as he became more similar to them. He envied them the one thing that he lacked and they possessed: the importance they were able to place on their lives, the amount of passion in their joys and fears, and the trepidation but sweet happiness of being constantly in love. These people were always in love with themselves, with women, with their children, with accolades or riches, and with aspirations. But this out of all things—the joy and foolishness of a child—was not what he learned from them. He learned, of all things, the unpleasant aspects that he himself despised. More and more frequently it happened such that, after having had guests the night before, he stayed in bed for a long time feeling tired and incapable of thought. He became angry and impatient when Kamaswami bored him with worries. He sometimes laughed just a bit too loudly when he lost a game of dice. His countenance was still more intelligent and spiritual than others, but it rarely laughed, and it began to assume one and then another of those features which are so often found in the faces of wealthy people: features of discontent, sickliness, ill-humor, sloth, or cold-heartedness. The disease of the soul which rich people have had slowly taken hold of him.

Fatigue had come slowly over Siddhartha like a veil or a fine mist; it became a bit denser every day, a bit murkier every month, a bit heavier each year. As a new dress in time becomes old, loses its beautiful color, gets stains and wrinkles, becomes worn at the seams, and becomes thread-bare in spots here or there, Siddhartha's new life after he separated from Govinda had become old, losing color and splendor as the years went by, or gathering wrinkles and stains, and showing ugliness here or there. Hidden at the bottom, disappointment and disgust were waiting; Siddhartha did not notice it. He noticed only that the bright and reliable voice inside of him that had awakened him in that time and had always guides him in his best times had become silent.

He had been captured by the world, by lust, covetousness, indolence, and ultimately by that vice which he had once despised and mocked as the most foolish of all the vices: greed. Property, possessions, and riches had also finally ensnared him; they were no longer the trifles of a game to him and had become a shackle and a burden. In some odd and devious way, Siddhartha had become trapped in this final and most base of all addictions by means of the game of dice. Siddhartha began to play the game for money and precious things when he stopped being a Samana in his heart; the game, which he at other times had joined only casually and with a smile, as if partaking in a custom of the childlike people, he now pursued with increasing rage and passion. He was a feared gambler, and so high and audacious were his stakes that few dared challenge him. He played the game because of the pain in his heart; wasting his wretched money on the game brought him ferocious joy. In no other way could he, more clearly and with more contempt, demonstrate his disdain for wealth, the false god of merchants. In this way he gambled mercilessly and with high stakes, hating and mocking himself. He won thousands and threw away thousands; he lost money, jewelry, a house in the country, and won them back, then lost them again. This terrible and petrifying fear, which he felt while rolling the dice and concerned about the high stakes, was something he loved and always sought to renew or increase. He always tried to raise it to a slightly higher level, because in this sensation alone did he still feel something akin to happiness, intoxication, or an elevated existence in the midst of his lukewarm, dull, and saturated life.

His mind was fixed upon new riches after each big loss, and he pursued trade more zealously, forced his debtors with greater stringency to pay; he wanted to continue gambling, squandering, and demonstrating his disdain for wealth. Siddhartha lost his equanimity when he lost a game, he became impatient when he was not paid promptly, he was no longer kind towards beggars, and he was no longer disposed to give away or even loan money to those who petitioned him. He who laughed at gambling away tens of thousands in one dice roll became stricter and pettier in his business dealings, even dreaming during the nights on occasion about money! Whenever he woke from this accursed ensorcellment, whenever he found himself aged and uglier when he saw his face in the mirror on the bedroom wall, and whenever embarrassment and disgust came over him, he continued fleeing into a new game or into the numbness of the mind brought on by sex and wine. From there, he fled back to the urge to hoard possessions. He ran in this pointless cycle as he grew old, tired, and sick.

Then came the time when a dream warned him. He had spent the evening hours with Kamala in her gorgeous pleasure garden. They had been sitting and talking beneath the trees, and Kamala had said pensive words behind which lay hidden sadness and fatigue. She had asked him to tell her about Gotama, and couldn't hear enough of him—how his eyes were clear, his mouth was still and beautiful, and how his smile was kind and his walk peaceful. He had told her about the exalted Buddha for a long time, and Kamala had sighed, saying: "Perhaps one day soon I'll also follow that Buddha. I'll give him my pleasure garden as a gift and take my refuge in his teachings."

After this, however, she had aroused him, tying him to her in the act of lovemaking with a painful fervor, amidst biting and tears, as if she once more wanted to squeeze the last drop out of this vain, fleeting pleasure. Never before had it become so oddly clear to Siddhartha how akin lust was to death. He had lain by Kamala's side, and her face was close to his; under her eyes and next to the corners of the mouth he read, as he had never clearly read before, a horrible inscription of small lines, slight grooves. It was an inscription reminiscent of the autumn time and old age, just like Siddhartha himself, had already noticed, in the gray hairs here and there among his black ones. Fatigue was written on Kamala's beautiful face, and exhaustion from walking a long path with no happy destination; it was a fatigue and the start of withering, along with the concealed and unspoken (perhaps even unconscious) fear of old age, of autumn, of death. With a sigh, he said farewell to her while his soul was full of hesitation and hidden anxiety.

Siddhartha then spent the night at his house with dancing girls and

wine, acting towards the other members of his caste as if he were superior
to them, even though this was no longer true. He had imbibed much wine
and went to bed long after midnight; he was tired and yet excited, and
was close to weeping and despair. He long sought sleep in vain, and his
heart was full of misery that he felt he could no longer bear; it was full of
a disgust that he felt penetrating his entire body like the lukewarm and
revolting taste of the wine, the music that was dull and all too sweet, the
all-too-soft smiles of the dancing girls, and the all-too-sweet scent of their
hair and breasts. More than anything else, however, he was disgusted with
himself: his perfumed hair, the smell of wine coming from his mouth, the
flabby fatigue and the listlessness of his skin. As is a man who has eaten
and drunk far too much, vomiting it back up again with agonizing pain
and being nevertheless glad for the relief, this sleepless man in an outburst
of disgust wanted to free himself from these pleasures and habits. He
wanted to free himself from this entire pointless life and from himself. It
was not until morning's light came and the first bustling of activity began
on the street near his city dwelling that he fell asleep; he had found for a
few moments a state of semi-unconsciousness, a hint of slumber. In these
moments, he had a dream:

Kamala owned a small, rare songbird in a golden cage. He dreamed
of this bird. He dreamed that this bird, which at other times used to sing
in the morning, had become mute. This attracted his attention, and he
stepped in front of the cage and looked inside. There lay the small bird,
stiff and dead on the floor. He took the bird out, weighed it for a moment
in his hand, and then threw it away into the street. In the same moment, he
felt terribly shocked, and his heart panged him, almost as if he had thrown
away from himself everything good or valuable by throwing out this
dead bird.

Awaking with a start from this dream, he felt enveloped by deep sadness. It seemed to him that the way he had been leading life was worthless
and pointless. Nothing was alive, and he had kept nothing in his hands
that was in any way delicious or worth keeping. He stood alone and empty,
like a castaway on the shore.

With gloomy thoughts, Siddhartha went to his pleasure garden. He
locked the gate, sat down under a mango tree, and felt death and in his
heart and horror in his chest. He sat and sensed how everything within him
had died, withered, and terminated. By and by he gathered his thoughts,
and in his mind he once again traveled his entire life's path, beginning
with the first days he could remember. Was there ever a time when he had
experienced happiness and felt true bliss? Certainly, he had experienced
such a thing several times. In his boyhood he had a taste of it when he

obtained praise from the Brahmins. He had then felt in his heart: "There is a path in front of the one who has distinguished himself in the recitation of the holy verses, in debates with the scholars, and as an assistant in the sacrifices." At that time he had felt in his heart: "There is a path in front of you, you have a destiny, and the gods are awaiting you." Once again, as a young man, the ever-ascendant and always-loftier goal of all contemplation had plucked him out from the masses who also sought the same goal, when with pain he wrestled for the sake of the Brahman, when every bit of knowledge he acquired only ignited new thirst within him, he had again felt this very same thing in the midst of the thirst and pain: "Go on! Go on! You have been called!" He had heard this voice when leaving his home and choosing the Samana's life, and again when he had left the Samanas to go to the perfected one, and also when he had departed from him into that which is uncertain. How long had it been that he did not hear this voice; for how long had he reached no heights? How monotonous was the way in which his path had coursed through life—without a goal, without thirst, without exultation for many long years, being content with small pleasures of lust and yet never satisfied! For all these many years, he had tried and longed, without knowing it himself, to become a man like all the many others, like the children. In all of this his life had been far more miserable and destitute than theirs. Neither their goals nor their worries were his; after all, the entire world of the Kamaswami-people had been only a game to him, a dance or a comedy that he would watch. Only Kamala had been dear and valuable to him—but was she still so? Did he still need her, or she him? Weren't they playing a game that had no end? Was it necessary to live for this? No, it was not necessary! The name of this game was Samsara, a game for children, which was enjoyable to play perhaps once, twice, or ten times—but again and again for ever and ever?

Siddhartha then knew that the game was over and that he could no longer play it. He felt shivers run over his body and inside of him; something had died.

He sat under the mango tree that entire day while thinking of his father, of Govinda, and of Gotama. Did he have to leave them to become a Kamaswami? When night fell he was still sitting there. When he caught sight of the stars while looking up, he thought: "Here I am sitting under my mango tree, in my pleasure garden." He smiled slightly—was it truly necessary or right, was it even like a foolish game, for him to own a mango tree, to own a garden?

He also put an end to this, and this died within him. He rose up, said farewell to the mango tree and to the pleasure garden. He felt very hungry because he had gone without food that day, and he thought of his house in the city, of his chamber and his bed, and of the table there and the meals upon it. He smiled tiredly, shook himself, and said goodbye to these things.

Siddhartha left his garden at that same hour during the night; he left the city and never came back. Kamaswami had people seek him for a long time, thinking that he had fallen into the hands of robbers. Kamala did not have anyone look for him. She was not astonished when told that Siddhartha had disappeared. Hadn't she always expected it? Wasn't he a Samana, a man who was nowhere at home, a pilgrim? And, most of all, she had sensed this the last time they had been together, and in spite of all the pain of loss she was happy that she had drawn him so affectionately to her heart for that last time, that she had felt once more so completely possessed and penetrated by him.

When she first received the news of Siddhartha's disappearance, she went to the window where she held a rare songbird captive in a golden cage. She opened the door of the cage, took out the bird, and let it fly. She gazed after the flying bird for a long time. She received no more visitors from this day forward, and she kept her house locked. After some time, however, she became aware that she was pregnant from that last time she was together with Siddhartha.

By the River

SIDDHARTHA WANDERED in the forest. He was already far from the city, and knew only that he could not return, that life as he had known it for many years was gone and had dwindled away until he was disgusted and bone-dry. Dead were the singing birds of his dreams. Dead was the bird in his heart. Deeply entangled in the Samsara was he, and revulsion and death had he absorbed from all sides, as a sponge absorbs water, until he was full. He was full of disgust, full of suffering, full of death, until nothing in the world allured him, gave him joy, or comforted him.

He wished ardently to no longer know of himself, to have quiet, to be dead. Would that the lightning would come to strike him! Would that the tiger would come and devour him! Would that there was a wine, a poison that could anesthetize him, bring him forgetfulness and a slumber from which there was no more awakening! Was there not still some smut with which he had not stained himself, a sin and foolishness that he had not committed, a lament of the soul with which he had not burdened himself? Was it then yet possible to live? Was it possible, once more and yet once more to draw breath, to expel breath, to feel hunger, once more to eat, once more to sleep, once more to lie down by a woman? Was not this cycle exhausted and completed?

Siddhartha reached the large river in the woods, the selfsame river over which he had once been lead by a ferryman when he was a younger man and came from the city of Gotama. On this river he stopped, hesitated, and remained standing by the shore. Fatigue and hunger had weakened

him, and to where should he travel further—where then, and to what goal?
No, there were no more goals. There remained only the deep, sorrowful
longing of the heart, remained only to shake off this whole arid dream of
his, to spit out this stale wine, to bring to an end this entire wretched and
ignominious life.

A tree hung over the riverbank, a coconut tree, and upon its branches
Siddhartha leaned his shoulder. He laid his arm on the branch and glanced
down under the green water that sluggishly passed by beneath him; he
looked beneath the surface and found himself wholly and totally con-
sumed by the desire to lose himself and to go beneath this water. He saw
a horrible emptiness escaping the water's reflection, to which the terrible
emptiness in his soul gave answer. Yes, it was the end. There was nothing
more for him other than to extinguish himself, to destroy the failure of
his life, to throw himself away before the feet of the scoffing and scornful
gods. This was the immense vomit that he had yearned for: the death, the
destruction of his hated corporeal form! He wanted the fish to feed upon
him, this dog Siddhartha, this madman, this corrupt and rotted body; this
limp and abused soul wanted the fish and the crocodiles to devour him,
wanted the demons to dismember him!

He stared into the water with a distorted face, saw his face reflected
there, and spat at the reflection. He took his arm away from the trunk of
the tree in deep fatigue and turned a bit in order to let himself fall straight
down and finally drown. With his eyes closed, he slipped towards death.

Then, out of the deep recesses of his soul and out of the past of his
now weary life, a sound stirred. It was a word, a syllable, and he, without
thinking and with a slurred voice, spoke to himself. It was the old word
which is the beginning and the end of all Brahmin prayers, the holy "Om,"
which means roughly "that which is perfect" or "the completion." In that
moment when the sound of "Om" touched Siddhartha's ear, his dormant
spirit suddenly awoke and realized the foolishness of his actions.

Siddhartha was deeply shocked. This was how things stood with him;
he was so doomed, so lost and forsaken by all knowledge, that he had been
able to seek death; this wish, the wish of a child, had been able to grow in
him: to find rest by annihilating his body! All the agony of recent times, all
the sobering realizations, all the desperation had not produced what was
now brought on by the moment when the "Om" entered his consciousness.
He became aware of himself in his misery and error.

He said to himself: "Om!" And again, "Om!" He knew again about
Brahman, about the indestructibility of life, about all that is divine and that
he had forgotten.

Yet this was only a momentary flash. Siddhartha collapsed by the foot of the coconut tree; he was struck down by fatigue. Mumbling "Om," he placed his head on the root of the tree and fell into a deep sleep.

His sleep was deep and dreamless; he had not known such sleep for a long time. When he awoke after many hours, he felt as if ten years had passed. He heard the water flowing quietly, and did not know where he was and who had brought him here. Opening his eyes, he saw with astonishment that there were trees and the sky above him, and he remembered where he was and how he had come there. This took a long while, and the past seemed infinitely distant, far away, and meaningless to him, as if it had been covered by a veil. He knew only that his previous life—in the first moment that he considered it, this past life seemed to him like an ancient pre-incarnation, like a proto-birth of his present self—had been abandoned by him, that, full of disgust and wretchedness, he had even intended to throw his life away. He had come to his senses, however, under a coconut tree by the river; with the holy word "Om" on his lips, he had fallen asleep and had now awakened, looking at the world as a new man. He had spoken the word "Om" quietly to himself, and, speaking it, he had fallen asleep; it seemed to him as if the entirety of his long sleep had been nothing but a long, meditative recitation of "Om," a thought of "Om," a submergence and complete entering into "Om," into the nameless perfection.

What a wonderful sleep this had been! He had never before been so refreshed by sleep, so renewed and rejuvenated! Perhaps he had really died; perhaps he had drowned and was reborn in a new body? But no—he knew himself, his hands and his feet and the place where he lay. He knew this self in his breast, this Siddhartha, the eccentric and strange one; this Siddhartha was nonetheless transformed, renewed, and—strangely—was well rested, awake, joyful, and curious.

Siddhartha straightened up, and saw a person sitting opposite him. He was an unknown man, a monk in a yellow robe and a shaved head who was sitting in the contemplative position. He observed this man who had neither hair on his head nor a beard, and he had not observed long before he recognized this monk as Govinda, the friend of his youth, who had taken his refuge with the exalted Buddha. Govinda had also aged, but his face still bore the same features: expressive zeal, faithfulness, seeking, and timidity. However, when Govinda, sensing Siddhartha's gaze, opened his eyes and looked at him, Siddhartha saw that Govinda did not now recognize him. Govinda was glad to find Siddhartha awake; apparently, he had been sitting there for a long time while waiting for him to wake up, even though he did not know him.

"I have been sleeping," said Siddhartha. "However did you get here?"

"You have been sleeping," answered Govinda. "It is not good to sleep in such places, where there are often snakes and where the paths of the forest animals are. I, dear sir, am a follower of the exalted Gotama, the Buddha, the Sakyamuni, and several of us have been on a pilgrimage together on this path when I saw you lying down and sleeping in a place where it is dangerous to sleep. I therefore sought to wake you up, dear sir, and since your sleep was very deep, I let the group go on ahead and sat with you. And so then it seems that I, who wanted to guard your sleep, have fallen asleep myself. I have done you a disservice, and fatigue has overwhelmed me. Now that you are awake, however, let me go catch up with my brothers.

"Thank you, Samana, for watching over my sleep," spoke Siddhartha. "You disciples of the exalted one are amiable. You may go now, then."

"I'm going, sir. May you always enjoy success."

"Thank you, Samana."

Govinda made a sign of greeting and said "Farewell."

"Farewell, Govinda," said Siddhartha.

The monk stopped.

"May I ask, sir, from where it is that you know my name?"

Siddhartha now smiled.

"I know you, O Govinda, from your father's hut and from the school of the Brahmins; I know you from the sacrifices and our walk to the Samanas, and from that hour when you took your refuge with the exalted one in the grove Jetavana."

"You're Siddhartha!" exclaimed Govinda loudly. "I now recognize you, and I don't understand how I hadn't recognized you immediately. Be welcome, Siddhartha; it is my great joy to see you again."

"It also gives me joy to see you again. You've been the guardian of my sleep; again I thank you for this, although I wouldn't have required any guardian. Where are you going, O friend?"

"I'm going nowhere. We monks always travel when it is not the rainy season; we always move from one place to another, always live according to the teachings passed on to us, accept alms, and then move on. It's always like this. But Siddhartha—where are you going?"

Siddhartha spoke: "It is the same with me, friend, as it is with you. I'm going nowhere. I'm just traveling. I'm on a pilgrimage."

Govinda spoke: "You say you're on a pilgrimage, and I believe you. But forgive me, O Siddhartha, you do not look like a pilgrim. You're wearing a wealthy man's clothes and the shoes of a distinguished gentleman, and your hair, which has the fragrance of perfume, is not a pilgrim's hair nor the hair of a Samana."

"Exactly, my good man; you have observed well and your keen eyes see everything. But I didn't say to you that I was a Samana. I said: I'm on a pilgrimage. And so it is: I'm on a pilgrimage."

"You're on a pilgrimage," said Govinda, "but few would go on a pilgrimage in such clothes, such shoes, and such hair. Never have I met such a pilgrim, having been a pilgrim myself for many years."

"I believe you, dear Govinda. Today, however, you've met a pilgrim just like this, wearing such shoes and such garments. Remember, my good man: the world of appearances is not eternal, and our garments, hairstyle, even our hair and bodies themselves are anything but eternal. I'm wearing a rich man's clothes; this you've quite rightly perceived. I'm wearing them because I have been a rich man, and I'm wearing my hair like the worldly, lust-filled people, for I have been one of them."

"And what, Siddhartha, are you now?"

"I don't know, just as you don't know. I'm traveling. I was a rich man and am not a rich man any more; what I'll be tomorrow, I don't know."

"You've lost your riches?"

"I've lost them or they lost me. They somehow happened to slip away from me. The wheel of physical manifestations is turning quickly, Govinda. Where is Siddhartha the Brahmin? Where is Siddhartha the Samana? Where is Siddhartha the rich man? Ephemeral things change quickly, Govinda; you know this."

Govinda looked for a long time with doubt in his eyes at the friend of his youth. After that, he gave him the greeting which one would use on a gentleman and went on his way.

With a smiling face, Siddhartha watched him leave. He still loved him, this faithful and fearful man. How could he not love everybody and everything in this moment, following the glorious hour after his wondrous sleep that was filled with "Om!" The very enchantment that had transpired inside of him during his sleep by means of "Om" was the fact that he loved everything, that he was full of joyous love for everything he saw. It was this very thing, it seemed to him now, which had been his sickness before: that he was not able to love anybody or anything.

Siddhartha had a smiling face as he watched the monk leave. The sleep had strengthened him greatly, but he had many hunger pains because he now hadn't eaten for two days, and the times when he had been hardened against hunger were now long gone. He thought of that time with sadness and yet also with a smile. He remembered that in those days he had boasted of three things to Kamala; he had been able to do three noble and insurmountable feats: fasting, waiting, and thinking. These had been his possession, his power and strength, his solid staff. In the busy and laborious years of his youth he had learned these three feats and nothing else. Now, they had abandoned him; none of them were his any more, neither fasting, nor waiting, nor thinking. He had given them up for the most wretched things, for that which fades most quickly: sensual lust, a life of luxury, and riches! His life had been strange indeed. And so it now seemed that he had truly become a childlike person.

Siddhartha thought about his situation. Thinking was difficult for him; he didn't really feel like doing it, and yet he forced himself.

Now that all these fleeting things have slipped away from me again, he thought, I'm standing here beneath the sun, just as I stood here as a little child. Nothing is mine. I can do nothing. I don't have the ability to do anything. I have learned nothing. How wondrous is all this! Now that I'm no longer young, with my hair already half-gray, with my strength fading, I'm starting as a child again at the beginning! He had to smile again. Yes, his destiny had been strange! Things had been going in a downward spiral for him, and now he faced the world again void, naked, and stupid. But he could not feel sad about this; instead, he even felt a great urge to laugh about himself and about this strange, foolish world.

"Things are going in a downward spiral for you!" he said to himself, and laughed about it. As he was saying this, he happened to glance at the river, and he saw that the river was also going downwards, always moving downhill while singing and being happy through it all. He liked this, and smiled kindly at the river. Wasn't this the same river in which he had intended to drown himself in former times, a hundred years ago, or had he dreamed that?

My life has been wondrous indeed, so he thought; it has taken wondrous detours. As a boy, I concerned myself only with gods and sacrifices. As a youth, I concerned myself only with asceticism, with thinking and meditation as I searched for Brahman and worshipped eternity in the Atman. But as a young man I followed the penitents, lived in the forest, suffered from heat and frost, learned to hunger, and taught my body to become dead. Insight came to me wonderfully in the form of the great Buddha's teachings. I felt the knowledge of the unity of the world coursing through me like my own blood. Yet I also had to leave the Buddha and the great knowledge. I went and learned the art of love with Kamala, learned to trade with Kamaswami, piled up money, wasted money, and learned to love my stomach and senses. It took me many years to lose my spirit, to unlearn thinking and forget the unity. Isn't it just as if I had turned about slowly and was on a long detour from being a man to being a child, from a thinker to a childlike person? And yet, this path has been very good, and the bird in my chest has not died. But what a path this has been! I had to pass through so much stupidity, so many vices, so many errors, so much disgust, so many disappointments and woes just to become a child again and to be able to begin again. But it was fitting this way; my heart says "Yes" to it and my eyes smile at it. I've had to experience despair. I've had to descend to the most foolish of all thoughts—the thought of suicide—in order to be able to experience divine grace, to hear "Om" again, to be able to sleep and awaken properly again. I had to become a fool to find Atman in me again. I had to sin to be able to live again. Where else might my path lead me? This path is foolish; it moves in loops, and perhaps it is going around in a circle. Let it go where it likes; I want to follow it.

Wonderfully, he felt joy swelling up within his breast.

From where, he asked his heart, from where did you get this happiness? Might it have come from that long, good sleep which has done me so much good? Or from the word "Om" which I said? Or perhaps from the fact that I have escaped, that I have completely fled, that I am finally free again and am standing like a child underneath the sky? Oh how good it is to have fled and to have become free! How clean and beautiful is the air here; how good it is to breathe it! Everything there where I escape from smelled like ointments, spices, wine, excess, and laziness. How I hated this world of the rich, of those who revel in fine food, of the gamblers! How did I hate myself for staying in this terrible world for so long! How I hated myself, deprived myself, poisoned and tortured myself, making myself old and evil! No, I will never again, as I used to like to do so much, delude myself into thinking that Siddhartha is wise! But I have done this one thing well; this pleases me and this I must praise: there is now an end to that self-hatred, that foolish and bleak life! I praise you, Siddhartha, for after so many years of foolishness, you have once again had a concept, you have done something, you have heard the bird in your breast singing and have followed it!

He praised himself in this way, found joy in himself, and listened with curiosity to his stomach, which was rumbling with hunger. He now felt as if he had in recent days fully tasted, spit out, and devoured a portion of suffering and misery, even to the point of desperation and death. And it was good. He could have stayed with Kamaswami for a lot longer, accruing money, wasting money, filling his stomach, and letting his soul die of thirst. He could have lived in this soft, upholstered hell for quite a bit longer if this moment had not happened, this moment of complete hopelessness and despair, that most extreme moment when he hung over the rushing waters, fully prepared to destroy himself. He felt joy because he had felt this despair and deep disgust and had not succumbed to it; he laughed because the bird, that joyful source and the voice within him was still alive after all. This was why his face was smiling brightly under his graying hair.

"It's good," he thought, "to taste for one's self all that which one needs to know. The lust for the world and wealth were not among the best things in life; I already learned this as a child. I have known it for a long time, but have only experienced this now. And now I know this, not just in my mind, but in my eyes, my heart, and my stomach. Bravo for me because I know this!"

He pondered his transformation for a long time; he listened to the bird as it sang for joy. Hadn't this bird died within him; hadn't he felt its death? No, something else within himself had died, something which he had yearned to see die for a long time. Wasn't it this thing that he had wanted to deaden in his years as a devout penitent? Wasn't it his small, frightened, and proud self, with which he had wrestled for so many years and which had defeated him time and again, coming back after every deadening, every forbidden joy, every troubled fear? Wasn't it this which had today finally come to its death in the forest by this lovely river? Was it not because of this death that he was now like a child, so trusting, fearless, and joyful?

Siddhartha now had some notion of why his fight against this self had been in vain while he was a Brahmin and a penitent. Too much knowledge had been holding him back, too many holy verses, sacrificial rules, self-castigation, and striving for this goal! He had always been full of arrogance, the most intelligent, the most zealous worker, one step ahead of the others, the knowing and spiritual one, the priest or the wise one. His self had retreated into this arrogance, this spirituality, this priesthood, and there it was firmly planted, growing, while he thought he would kill it by fasting and penance. Now he saw it, and saw that the secret voice had been correct, that no teacher would have ever been able to bring about his salvation. This was why he had gone out into the world to lose himself to lust and power, to women and money. He had had to become a merchant, a gambler with the dice, a drunkard, and a miser until the priest and Samana within him were dead. This is why he had to endure these hated years—the revulsion, the lessons, the pointlessness of a dreary and wasted life—endure up to the end, up to bitter despair, until Siddhartha the lust-filled and greedy one could also die. He had died, and a new Siddhartha had awakened out of the sleep. He would also grow old and eventually have to die; Siddhartha was mortal, and every physical form was mortal. But today he was young and a child; he was the new Siddhartha and was full of joy.

He contemplated these thoughts and perked up his ears with a smile at his grumbling stomach, and listened with thanks to the buzzing bee. He looked cheerfully into the rushing river; he had never before had water so please him, never had he perceived the voice and parable of the moving water so strongly and beautifully. It seemed to him as if the river had something special to tell him that he did not yet know; it was still awaiting him. Siddhartha had intended to drown himself in this river, and the old, tired, desperate Siddhartha had drowned today. But the new Siddhartha felt a deep love for this rushing water, and decided on his own not to leave it any time soon.

The Ferryman

I WANT TO STAY by this river, thought Siddhartha; it is the same one that I crossed long ago on my way to the childlike people. A friendly ferryman guided me then; he is the one to whom I want to go. Beginning from his hut, my path at that time led me to a new life which has now grown old and dead. My present path and new life shall also have its start there!

He looked tenderly into the rushing water, the transparent green, the crystal lines of this secret-filled sketch. He saw bright pearls rising from the deep and quiet bubbles of air floating on the reflective surface that had the blue sky depicted upon it. The river looked at him with a thousand eyes: green ones, white ones, crystal ones, sky-blue ones. How he loved this water, how it delighted him, and how grateful he was to it! He heard the voice talking in his heart; it had awakened anew, and it told him: Love this water! Stay near it! Learn from it! Ah yes, he wanted to learn from it and listen to it. It seemed to him that he would understand this water and its secrets, and would also understand many other things, many secrets and all secrets.

But out of all the secrets of the river, he saw only one today, and it touched his soul. He saw that this water ran and ran incessantly, and nevertheless was always there at all times, the same and yet new every moment! The one who grasped this and understood this was great! He did not understand and grasp it, but felt some inkling of it stirring, a distant memory and divine voices.

Siddhartha rose up, and the hunger of his body became unbearable.

He walked in a daze, up the path by the bank and up-river. He listened to the current and listened to the rumbling hunger in his body.

The boat was just ready when he reached the ferry, and the same ferryman who had once transported the young Samana across the river now stood in the boat. Siddhartha recognized him, and he had aged quite a bit.

"Do you want to ferry me over?" asked Siddhartha.

The ferryman, astonished to see such an elegant man walking along on foot, took him into his boat and pushed off from the bank.

"This is a beautiful life that you've chosen for yourself," said the passenger. "It must be beautiful to live by the water every day and to move about upon it."

The man at the oar moved it from side to side with a smile: "It is beautiful, sir, as you say. But isn't every life and every work beautiful?"

"This may be true, but I envy you yours."

"Ah, you would stop enjoying it soon. This is no work for people who wear fine clothes."

Siddhartha laughed. "I have already been looked upon once today with mistrust because of my clothes. Wouldn't you, ferryman, like to take these bothersome clothes from me? For, I'll have you know, I have no money to pay your fare."

"You're joking, sir!" laughed the ferryman.

"I'm not joking, friend. See, you have already ferried me across this water once before, and did it only out of love. Do this again today, and accept my clothes in exchange for it."

"And do you, sir, intend to travel on your way without clothes?"

"Eh, I would much prefer not to travel any farther at all. I would most like it if, ferryman, you were to give me an old loincloth and keep me with you as your assistant, or rather as your apprentice, because first I'll have to learn how to handle the boat."

The ferryman looked at the stranger searchingly for a long time.

"I recognize you now," he finally said. "You slept in my hut once a long time ago, possibly more than twenty years ago. I ferried you across the river and we parted like good friends. Weren't you a Samana? I can't recall what your name is any more."

"My name is Siddhartha, and I was a Samana when last you saw me."

"Welcome, then, Siddhartha. My name is Vasudeva. You will, I hope, be my guest today and sleep in my hut as well, and tell me where you're coming from and why these beautiful clothes are such a bother to you."

They had reached the middle of the river, and Vasudeva used more strength to push the oar so that he could overcome the current. He worked his brawny arms calmly, fixing his eyes on the front of the boat. Siddhartha sat and watched him, remembering how, once before on his last day as a Samana, he had felt love for this man stir in his heart. He gratefully accepted Vasudeva's invitation. When they had reached the bank, Siddhartha helped him tie the boat to the stakes; after this, the ferryman asked Siddhartha to enter the hut; the ferryman then offered Siddhartha bread and water, and Siddhartha ate eagerly and with pleasure. He also eagerly ate with pleasure the mango fruits that Vasudeva offered him.

Afterwards, around sunset, they both sat on a log by the riverbank, and Siddhartha told the ferryman about where he originally came from. He also told him about his life as he had seen it before his eyes today in that hour of despair. His tale lasted late into the night.

Vasudeva listened with great attention. He let everything enter his mind as he listened carefully: birthplace and childhood, and all the learning, searching, joy, and distress. This among all the ferryman's virtues was one of the greatest: he knew how to listen as few others could. Without his saying a word, the speaker could sense how Vasudeva let words enter his mind, how he was quiet, open, and waiting, and how he did not lose a single word by impatience. He did not add his praise or rebuke, and simply listened. Siddhartha felt quite fortunate to be able to confess to a listener like this, to immerse his own life, his own search, and his own suffering in his heart.

Yet at the end of Siddhartha's tale, when he spoke about the tree by the river, about his deep fall, the holy "Om," and how he had felt great love for the river after his slumber, the ferryman listened with twice as much attention. He was entirely and completely absorbed by it, and his eyes were closed.

But then Siddhartha fell silent and there was a long pause; Vasudeva then said: "It is as I thought. The river has spoken to you. It is your friend, too; it speaks to you as well. That is good, very good. Stay with me, Siddhartha, my friend. I used to have a wife, and her bed was next to mine, but she died a long time ago and I have lived alone for a long time. Now you shall live with me; there is space and food for both of us.

"I thank you," said Siddhartha, "I thank you and accept. I also thank you for this, Vasudeva: for listening to me so well! People who know how to listen are rare, and I have never met a single one who could do this as well as you did. I would also like to learn from you in this regard."

"You will learn it," said Vasudeva, "but not from me. The river has taught me to listen, and you will learn it from the river as well. The river knows everything, and everything can be learned from it. See, you've already learned this from the water: that it is good to strive downwards, to sink and to seek depth. The rich and elegant Siddhartha is becoming an oarsman's servant, and the learned Brahmin Siddhartha is becoming a fer-ryman. This also has been told to you by the river. You'll learn that other thing from it as well."

After a long pause, Siddhartha said: "What other thing, Vasudeva?"

Vasudeva arose. "It's late," he said. "Let's go to sleep. I can't tell you that other thing, O friend. You'll learn it, or perhaps you know it already. See, I'm no scholar. I have no special skill in speaking or thinking. I only understand listening and piety; I've learned nothing else. If I were able to say and teach this, I might be a wise man, but as it stands I am only a ferryman, and it is my task to ferry people across the river. I have trans-ported many people—thousands—and for all these, my river has been nothing more than an obstacle in their travels. They travel seeking money and business, and for weddings and pilgrimages, and the river obstructs their path, and it is the job of the ferryman to get them quickly across this obstacle. But for a few among the thousands—four or five—the river has stopped becoming an obstacle. They have heard its voice and listened to it, and the river has become as sacred to them as it is to me. Let's rest now, Siddhartha."

Siddhartha stayed with the ferryman and learned how to operate the boat. When there was nothing to do at the ferry, he worked with Vasudeva in the rice field, gathered wood, and plucked fruit from the banana trees. He learned how to build an oar, mend the boat, and weave baskets. He was joyful because of all the things he learned, and the days and months passed quickly. But the river taught him more than Vasudeva could teach him. He learned from it incessantly. Above all, he learned to listen from it. He learned to pay attention closely with a quiet heart, with patience, and with an open soul devoid of passion, wishes, judgment, and opinions.

He lived side by side with Vasudeva in a friendly way, and they occa-sionally exchanged words that were few and well-considered. Vasudeva was no friend of words; it was rare that Siddhartha succeeded in persuad-ing him to speak.

"Have you," Siddhartha once asked him, "also learned the following secret from the river: that there is no time?"

Vasudeva's face was filled with a bright smile.

"Yes, Siddhartha," he said. "It is even this that you mean: the river is everywhere at once, at the source and the mouth, at the waterfall, the ferry, the rapids, the sea, and the mountains. It is everywhere at once, and there only the present exists for it—not the shadow of the past nor the shadow of the future."

"This is it," said Siddhartha. "And when I learned it, I looked at my

life and found that it also was a river, and that the boy Siddhartha was
separated from the man Siddhartha and the old man Siddhartha by only a
shadow, and not by something real. Siddhartha's previous births were also
no past, and his death and subsequent return to Brahman was no future.
Nothing was and nothing will be; everything is, and everything is present
and has existence."

Siddhartha spoke with ecstasy; this enlightenment had deeply
delighted him. Ah, were not all sufferings then time, and were not all
self-torments and personal fears time? Weren't all the difficult and hos-
tile things in the world gone and overcome as soon as one had overcome
time, and as soon as time could be thrust out of the mind? He had spoken
with ecstatic delight. Vasudeva, however, just smiled at him brightly and,
nodding silently in confirmation, he brushed his hand over Siddhartha's
shoulder and turned back to his work.

Once more, when the river had just swelled in the rainy season and
made powerful noise, Siddhartha said: "Isn't it the case, O friend, that the
river has a great multitude of voices? Doesn't it have the voice of a king, a
warrior, a bull, a nocturnal bird, a woman giving birth, a sighing person,
and a thousand other voices besides?"

"It is so," Vasudeva nodded. "The voices of all creatures are in
its voice."

"And do you know," continued Siddhartha, "what word it speaks when
you succeed in hearing all ten thousand of its voices at once?"

Vasudeva's face was smiling happily; he bent over to Siddhartha and
spoke the holy "Om" into his ear. And this had been the very thing which
Siddhartha also had been hearing.

And from time to time, Siddhartha's smile became more similar to the
ferryman's. It also became bright, also was suffused with bliss, also shone
out of a thousand small wrinkles, was also like a child's and was also like
an old man's. Many travelers, upon seeing the two ferrymen, thought they
were brothers. They both often sat together in the evening by the riverbank
on the log, saying nothing and listening to the water, which for them was
no water but the voice of life which exists and is forever taking shape. From
time to time, it happened that while they were listening to the river, they
thought of the same things: a conversation from the day before yesterday,
one of the travelers whose face and fate had occupied their thought, death,
or their childhood. They both looked at each other in the same moment
when the river had been saying something good to them. They looked at
each other, both thinking precisely the same thing, both delighted about
the same answer to the same question.

Something about this ferry and the two ferrymen was transmitted to others, and many travelers felt it. It occasionally happened that a traveler, having looked at the face of one of the ferrymen, began to tell the story of his life, recounting pains, confessing evil, and asking for comfort and advice. Occasionally, someone asked permission to stay with them for the night and listen to the river. Curious people also came, having been told that there were two wise men, or sorcerers, or holy men living by the ferry. The curious ones asked many questions, but they received no answers, and found neither sorcerers nor wise men, but only two friendly little old men who seemed mute and to have become a little strange and batty. The curious people then laughed, discussing how foolish and gullible were the common people who spread such vacuous rumors.

The years passed, and nobody counted them. Then, one time, monks came by on a pilgrimage. They were followers of Gotama, the Buddha, and were asking to be ferried across the river. They told the ferrymen that they were hurrying back to their great teacher, for news had spread that the exalted one was deathly ill and would soon die his last human death so that he might enter salvation. It was not long before a new flock of monks came by on their pilgrimage, and yet another, and not only the monks but most of the other travelers and people walking through the land spoke of nothing else but Gotama and his impending death. And, like people who stream from all directions and sides when they are going to war or a coronation, gathering like ants in swarms, they flocked as if drawn by a magic spell to the place where the great Buddha awaited his death, where that monumental event was going to take place and the great perfected one of an era was to become one with glory.

In those days, Siddhartha often thought about the dying wise man, the great teacher whose voice had exhorted nations and awakened hundreds of thousands, and whose voice Siddhartha had also once heard and whose holy face he had looked upon with reverence. He thought kindly of the Buddha, and saw his path to perfection before his eyes, remembering with a smile those words which he had said at one time when he was a young man to the exalted one. It seemed to him that they had been proud and precocious words, and he remembered them with a smile. He had long known that there was nothing separating him from Gotama any more, although Siddhartha was still unable to accept his teachings. No, there were no teachings that a person who truly sought and wanted to find could accept. But the one who had already found could approve of any teachings, every path and goal; there was nothing that stood between him and the other thousands who lived in the eternal and breathed that which is divine.

On one of those days when so many were going on a pilgrimage to the dying Buddha, Kamala, who was once the most beautiful of the courtesans, also went to him. She had retired from her previous life long ago, and had given her garden to the monks of Gotama as a gift, taking refuge in the teachings. She was among the friends and benefactors of pilgrims. Together with the boy Siddhartha, her son, she had embarked on foot in simple clothes because of the news of the coming death of Gotama. She traveled by the river with her little son, but the boy soon became tired, desiring to return home, rest, and eat. He became disobedient and started to whine.

Kamala often had to take a rest with him; he was accustomed to getting what he wanted from her. She had to feed him, comfort him, and scold him. He didn't understand why he had to go on this exhausting and tragic pilgrimage with his mother to an unknown place, to a stranger who was holy and about to die. What did it matter to the boy if he died?

The pilgrims approached Vasudeva's ferry when Siddhartha once again forced his mother to rest. Kamala herself had also become tired, and while the boy chewed on a banana, she crouched down on the ground, closed her eyes for a bit, and rested. But she suddenly uttered a wailing scream; the boy looked at her in fear and saw her face grow pale with horror; from beneath her dress fled a small black snake which had bitten Kamala.

They both now hurried along the path and came near the ferry, where Kamala collapsed, unable to go any further. The boy started to cry miserably, interrupting this only to kiss and hug his mother. She also joined his loud screams for help until the sound reached the ears of Vasudeva, who stood at the ferry. He came walking quickly, took the woman in his arms, and carried her into the boat. The boy ran along, and they all soon reached the hut where Siddhartha was standing by the stove and lighting the fire. He looked up and saw the boy's face, which oddly reminded him of something he had forgotten. Then he saw Kamala, whom he instantly recognized even though she was laying unconscious in the ferryman's arms. He now knew that it was his own son whose face had been a reminder to him, and his heart stirred within his breast.

They washed Kamala's wound, but it had already turned black and her body was swollen; she was administered a healing potion. Her consciousness returned, and she lay on Siddhartha's bed in the hut; Siddhartha, who once loved her so much, now stood bent over her. It seemed like a dream to her. With a smile, she looked at her friend's face. Slowly realizing her situation and remembering the bite, she called timidly for the boy.

"He's with you; don't worry," said Siddhartha.

Kamala looked into his eyes. She spoke with a thick tongue that was paralyzed by the poison. "You've become old, my love," she said. "You've become gray. But you are like the young Samana who once came to me in the garden without clothes and with dusty feet. You are much more like him than you were in the days when you left Kamaswami and me. You are like him in the eyes, Siddhartha. Alas, I have also become old...old—could you still recognize me?"

Siddhartha smiled. "I recognized you instantly, Kamala, love."

Kamala pointed to her boy and said: "Did you recognize him as well? He is your son."

Her eyes became confused and closed shut. The boy wept, and Siddhartha took him up on his knees, letting him weep and petting his hair. At the sight of the child's face, a Brahminic prayer came to his mind which he had learned a long time ago as a little boy himself. He started to speak slowly, with a singing voice; the words came flowing to him from his past and childhood. With that song, the boy became calm, uttering a sob only now and then and then falling asleep. Siddhartha placed him on Vasudeva's bed. Vasudeva stood by the stove and cooked rice. Siddhartha gave him a look which he returned with a smile.

"She'll die," Siddhartha said quietly.

Vasudeva nodded; the light of the stove's fire washed over his face.

Kamala returned to consciousness once more. Pain contorted her face, and Siddhartha's eyes read the suffering on her mouth and pale cheeks. He read it quietly and attentively, waiting, his mind becoming one with her suffering. Kamala felt it, and her gaze sought his eyes.

Looking at him, she said: "I now see that your eyes have changed as well. They've become completely different. By what means do I still recognize that you're Siddhartha? It's you, and yet it's not you."

Siddhartha said nothing; his eyes looked quietly at hers.

"You've achieved it?" she asked. "You have found peace?"

He smiled and placed his hand on hers.

"I see it," she said. "I see it. I, too, will find peace."

"You have found it," said Siddhartha in a whisper.

Kamala never stopped looking into his eyes. She thought about the pilgrimage that she wanted to take to Gotama, a pilgrimage to see the face of the perfected one, to breathe his peace; she then considered that, instead of him, she found Siddhartha, and that it was just as good as if she had seen Gotama. She wanted to tell Siddhartha this, but her tongue no longer obeyed her will. She looked at him without speaking, and he saw the life fade from her eyes. When the final pain filled her eyes and made them grow dim, when the final shiver ran through her limbs, his finger closed her eyelids.

He sat and looked for a long time at her sleeping face. He observed for a long time her old, tired mouth, with those lips that had become thin, and he remembered that, in the springtime of his years, he had compared this mouth to a freshly cracked fig. He sat for a long time, filling himself with this sight, and read his own face in the pale visage and tired wrinkles; it was just as white, just as extinguished. He saw his face and hers at the same time as they were young, with red lips, fiery eyes. The feeling of all this being both present and real, the feeling of eternity, completely filled every aspect of his being. He felt in this hour, more deeply than ever before, that every life was indestructible, that every moment was eternity.

When he rose up, Vasudeva had prepared rice for him. Siddhartha, however, did not eat. The two old men prepared beds of straw for themselves in the stable where their goat stood, and Vasudeva lay himself down to sleep. Siddhartha, however, went outside on this night and sat before the hut, listening to the river. He was surrounded by the past and was touched and enveloped by all the times of his life at once. He occasionally stood up, stepped into the door of the hut, and listened to see whether the boy was sleeping.

Vasudeva came out of the stable early in the morning, before the sun could be seen. He walked over to his friend.

"You haven't slept," he said.

"No, Vasudeva. I sat here listening to the river. It has told me quite a bit, and has deeply filled me with that healing thought of unity."

"You have experienced suffering, Siddhartha, but I see that no sadness has entered your heart."

"No, dear friend; how should I be sad? I, who have been rich and happy, have become even richer and happier now. My son has been given to me."

"Your son shall also be welcome to me. But let's get to work now, Siddhartha; there is much to be done. Kamala has died on the same bed upon which my wife died long ago. Let us also build Kamala's funeral pyre on the same hill where I then built my wife's funeral pyre."

They built the funeral pyre while the boy was still asleep.

The Son

T HE BOY, TIMID and weeping, attended his mother's funeral. He was shy and gloomy while listening to Siddhartha, who greeted him as his own son and welcomed him into his place in Vasudeva's hut. Pale, he sat by the hill of the dead for many days. He didn't want to eat, showed a stony countenance, closed his heart, and met his fate with resistance and denial.

Siddhartha went easy on him, letting the boy do as he pleased; Siddhartha honored his mourning. Siddhartha understood that his son did not know him, and that he could not love him like a father. He slowly saw and also understood that the eleven-year-old boy was pampered, that he was a mother's boy, and that he had grown up with the habits of wealthy people. He was accustomed to fine food, a soft bed, and servants to whom he could give orders. Siddhartha understood that the pampered child who was mourning could not suddenly and willingly be content with a poor life among strangers. He did not force him, did many chores for him, and always picked the best portion of the meal for him. He hoped to slowly win the boy over with kind patience.

He had called himself rich and happy when the boy had come to him. Time had passed in the meantime, and the boy was still a stranger and was still despondent. Siddhartha began to understand that his son had not brought him happiness and peace, but suffering and worry, when he saw that his son displayed a proud and stubbornly disobedient heart, didn't want to do any work, did not respect the old men, and stole from Vasudeva's fruit trees. And yet Siddhartha loved him, and preferred the suffering and worries of love over happiness and joy without the boy. Since young Siddhartha came to the hut, the old men had split the work. Vasudeva had once again taken on the job of ferryman all by himself, and Siddhartha, in order to be with his son, did the work in the hut and field.

Siddhartha waited for a long time—many months—to see his son understand him, accept his love, or perhaps reciprocate it. Vasudeva watched and waited for long months, and said nothing. One day, when the young Siddhartha had once again greatly tormented his father with spite and vacillation, breaking both of his rice bowls, Vasudeva took his friend aside in the evening and talked to him.

"Excuse me," he said, "but I'm talking to you from a heart full of cama-raderie. I'm watching you torment yourself, and I see that you're grieving. Your son, my friend, is worrying both you and me. That young bird is accustomed to a different life, to a different nest. He did not run away from riches and the city as you did when you were disgusted and fed up with it. He had to leave all this behind against his will. I have asked the river many times, my friend, about this. But the river laughs at me. It is laughing at you and me, and is shaking with laughter at our foolishness. Water wants to join water, youth wants to join youth—your son is not in a place where he can prosper. You, too, should ask the river; you should listen to it as well!

Troubled, Siddhartha looked into that friendly face, into the numerous wrinkles which held incessant cheerfulness within them.

"How could I part with him?" he said quietly, ashamed. "Give me some more time, my friend! I'm struggling for him, you see; I'm seeking to win his heart with love and kind patience, and I intend to capture it. The river shall also talk to him one day; he has also been called."

Vasudeva's smile blossomed even more fully. "Oh yes, he too is called, and he too is a part of the eternal life. But do we—you and I—know what he is called upon to do, what path he is to take, which actions he should perform, and which pains he should endure? His pain will not be slight; after all, his heart is hard and proud, and people like this have to suffer quite a bit, make many mistakes, do a great deal of injustice, and burden themselves with a lot of sin. Tell me, my friend: you're not disciplining your son? You don't force him? You don't beat him or punish him?"

"No, Vasudeva, I don't do any of these things."

"I knew it. You don't force him, beat him, and give him orders because you know that "soft" is stronger than "hard," that water is stronger than the rocks, that love is stronger than compulsion. This is good; I praise you. But aren't you mistaken in thinking that you aren't already forcing him or punishing him? Don't you shackle him with your love? Don't you, every day, make him feel inferior, and make it harder on him with your kindness and patience? Don't you force the arrogant and pampered boy to live in a hut with two old banana-eaters for whom even rice is a delicacy, whose thoughts can't be like his, and whose hearts are old and quiet and beating at a different pace from his? Isn't he coerced and punished by all this?

Troubled, Siddhartha looked at the ground. He quietly asked: "What do you think I should do?"

Vasudeva said: "Bring him to the city, take him to his mother's house, and give him to the servants who will still be around. If there aren't any that are still around, take him to a teacher, not for the sake of the teachings, but so that he will be among other boys and girls in a world which is his own. Haven't you ever thought about this?"

"You're seeing into my heart," said Siddhartha sadly. "I have often thought about this. But see, how am I going to put him, who doesn't have a tender heart anyway, into this world? Won't he become enthusiastic, lose himself to pleasure and power, repeat all of his father's mistakes, and get entirely lost in Samsara?"

The ferryman's smile lit up brightly. He softly touched Siddhartha's arm and said: "Ask the river about it, my friend! Hear it laugh about it! Do you actually believe that you committed your foolish acts in order to spare your son from committing them, too? How could you in any way protect your son from Samsara? How could you? Through prayers, lessons, and admonition? My friend, have you entirely forgotten that story about Siddhartha, a Brahmin's son, that contains so many lessons and which you once told me here on this very spot? Who kept Siddhartha the Samana safe from Samsara, sin, greed, and foolishness? Were his father's religious devotion, his teacher's warnings, his own knowledge, or his own seeking able to keep him safe? Which father or teacher was able to protect him from living his life for himself, soiling himself with life, burdening himself with guilt, drinking the bitter drink for himself, or finding this path for himself? Do you think, my friend, that anyone is spared from this path? That, perhaps, your little son would be spared because you love him and want to keep him from suffering, pain, and disappointment? But even if you would die ten times for him, you would not be able to take even the slightest part of his destiny upon yourself.

Vasudeva had never before spoken so many words. Siddhartha kindly thanked him, going into the hut full of trouble where he could not sleep for some time. Vasudeva had not told him anything that he hadn't already thought or known himself. But this knowledge was something he could not act upon, and stronger than this knowledge was his love for the boy, his tenderness, and his fear of losing him. Had he ever given his heart over so much to something? Had he ever loved anyone like this: blindly, unsuccessfully, in suffering—and yet still happy?

Siddhartha could not heed his friend's advice; he couldn't give up the boy. He allowed the boy to give him orders and disrespect him. He said nothing and waited, beginning each day to wage the mute battle of friendliness, the silent war of patience. Vasudeva also said nothing and waited, being friendly, wise, and patient. They were both masters of patience.

Once, when the boy's face reminded him very much of Kamala, Siddhartha suddenly recalled something which Kamala said to him long ago in the days of their youth. "You cannot love," she said to him; he had agreed with her, comparing himself with a star while likening the childlike people to falling leaves. He had, nevertheless, sensed accusation in that line. Indeed, he had never been able to lose himself or devote himself completely to another person, forgetting himself and committing foolish acts for the love of another person. He had never been able to do this, and it had seemed to him at the time that this was the great distinction that set him apart from the childlike people. But since his son had come, Siddhartha had also become a childlike person who suffered for the sake of another person, loved another person, lost himself to a love and became a fool because of love. He, too, now felt for once in his life this strongest and strangest of all passions; late in life he suffered miserably and was nevertheless in bliss, renewed in some sense, and enriched by a single thing.

He sensed quite strongly that this blind love for his son was a passion, something very human—that it was Samsara, a murky spring of dark waters. At the same time, he felt nonetheless that it was not worthless but necessary, that it came from the essence of his own being. This pleasure also must be atoned for, the pain also had to be endured, and these foolish acts also had to be committed.

Throughout all of this, the son let him commit foolish acts, let him court his affection while Siddhartha humiliated himself every day by giving in to the boy's moods. This father had nothing that delighted him and nothing that he feared. This father was a good man: kind, soft, perhaps very devout or a saint—and yet he had no traits which could win the boy over. This father, who kept him prisoner here in this miserable hut of his, was boring. He answered every naughtiness with a smile, every insult with amiability, every vicious comment with kindness; these were the abominable tricks of this sly old man. The boy would have liked it much more if the man had threatened or abused him.

The day came when the things on the young Siddhartha's mind came exploding forth, and he openly turned on his father. The latter had given the boy a task: he had told him to gather brushwood. The boy, however, did not leave the hut. He stayed where he was in stubborn disobedience and rage, thumped on the ground with his feet, clenched his fists, and screamed out in his father's face with an outburst filled with powerful hatred and contempt.

"Get the brushwood for yourself!" shouted the boy, foaming at the mouth. "I'm not your servant. I do know, however, that you won't dare hit me; I know that you constantly want to punish me and subdue me with your religious devotion and indulgence. You want me to become just as devout, soft, and wise as you! But listen up—just to make you suffer, I would rather become a highway robber and murderer, and go to hell, than to become like you! I hate you! You're not my father, even if you've been my mother's lover ten times over!"

Rage and grief frothed over within the boy as he foamed at the father with a hundred savage and evil words. The boy then ran away and returned only late at night.

But when the next morning came, he had disappeared. What had also disappeared was a small basket woven from raffia of two colors; this was where the ferrymen kept the copper and silver coins which they received as fare. The boat had also disappeared; Siddhartha saw it lying on the opposite bank. The boy had run away.

"I must follow him," said Siddhartha, who had been shaking with grief since the boy's ranting and raving yesterday. "A child can't go through the forest all alone. He'll perish. We have to build a raft, Vasudeva, and cross over the water."

"We'll build a raft," said Vasudeva, "so that we can get back the boat which the boy has taken away. But you should let the boy run along, my friend. He is no longer a child; he knows how to get around. He's looking for the path to the city, and he is doing what is correct: don't forget that. He's doing what you've failed to do yourself. He's taking care of himself; he's following his path. Alas, I see you suffering, Siddhartha, but you're suffering a pain which is somewhat laughable, and at which you'll soon be laughing yourself."

Siddhartha gave no answer. He already held the axe in his hands, and he began to make a raft of bamboo; Vasudeva helped him tie the canes together with grass ropes. They then crossed over, drifting far off their course and landing the raft upriver on the opposite bank.

"Why did you bring the axe?" asked Siddhartha.

Vasudeva said: "It could be that our boat's oar became lost."

Siddhartha knew what his friend was really thinking. He was thinking that the boy threw the oar away or broke it to avenge himself and keep

them from following him. And, in fact, there was no oar left in the boat.
Vasudeva pointed at the bottom of the boat and looked at his friend, smiling, as if to say: "See what your son is trying to tell you? Can't you see that
he doesn't want to be followed?" He didn't say this with words, however.
Vasudeva started making a new oar. Siddhartha, however, said farewell and
then went to look for the runaway. Vasudeva didn't stop him.

After Siddhartha had already been walking through the forest for a
long time, it occurred to him that his search was futile. Either the boy was
far ahead and had already reached the city, he thought, or he is still on his
way, concealing himself from the pursuer. As he continued to think, he also
found that he was not worried about his son, and knew deep inside that
his son neither had perished nor was in any danger in the forest. Even so,
he ran without stopping—not to save the boy, but just to satisfy his desire
to see him once more. He ran until he was just outside the city.

When he reached a wide road near the city, he stopped by the entrance
of the beautiful pleasure garden which once belonged to Kamala and where
he had seen her in her sedan chair for the first time. The past welled up
within his soul, and he once again saw himself standing there as a young,
bearded, naked Samana with a hair full of dust. Siddhartha stood there
for a long time and looked through the open gate into the garden, seeing
monks in yellow robes walking among the beautiful trees.

He stood there contemplating things for a long time, seeing visions
and listening to his life's story. He stood there for a long time as he looked
at the monks and saw instead a young Siddhartha and a young Kamala
walking among the high trees. He clearly saw himself being served food
and drink by Kamala, receiving his first kiss from her, and looking proudly
and scornfully back on Brahminism as he began his worldly life full of
desire and pride. He saw Kamaswami, the servants, the banquets, the gamblers with their dice, the musicians, Kamala's songbird in its cage. He lived
through all of this once again, breathing Samsara; he was old and tired
once again, felt disgust once again, and once again wanted to annihilate
himself and be healed by the holy "Om".

After standing at the garden's gate for a long time, Siddhartha realized
that the desire that made him come to this place was foolish. He could not
help his son, and he was not allowed to cling to him. He felt love for the
runaway deep within his heart like a wound. At the same time, he felt that
this wound had not been given to him so that he could turn a knife in it;
the wound must blossom and shine.

The fact that this wound had not yet blossomed and did not yet shine
made him sad at this hour. Instead of the goal of seeing his runaway son
that had drawn him here, there was now emptiness. Filled with sadness,

he sat down; he felt something dying in his heart and felt empty, no longer seeing any joy and having no goal. He was lost in thought as he sat and waited. He had learned this one thing by the river: how to wait, how to have patience, how to listen attentively. He sat and listened while sitting in the dust of the road. He listened to his heart as it beat tiredly and sadly, and he waited for a voice. He crouched and listened for many hours, but saw no visions any more. He fell into emptiness, and let himself fall without seeing a path. When he felt this wound burning, he silently spoke the Om and filled himself with Om. The monks in the garden saw him, and since he was crouching for many hours and dust was gathering on his gray hair, one of them came to him and placed two bananas in front of him. The old man did not see him.

He awoke from this petrified state by the touch of a hand on his shoulder. He instantly recognized this tender, bashful, touch, and he regained his senses. He rose up and greeted Vasudeva, who had followed him. When he looked into Vasudeva's friendly face, saw the small wrinkles filled with nothing but his smile, and saw his happy eyes, Siddhartha smiled, too. He now saw the bananas lying in front of him, picked them up, and gave one to the ferryman, eating the other one himself. After this, he silently went back into the forest with Vasudeva and returned home to the ferry. Neither one talked about what had happened today, neither one mentioned the boy's name, neither one spoke about his running away, and neither one spoke about the wound. Siddhartha lay down on his bed inside the hut, and after a while when Vasudeva came to offer him a bowl of coconut-milk, the ferryman found Siddhartha already asleep.

"*Om*"

SIDDHARTHA'S WOUND continued to burn for a long time. He had to ferry many travelers accompanied by their sons or daughters across the river, and there wasn't one that he saw without envy, thinking: "So many thousands possess this sweetest of good fortunes. Why don't I? Even evil people—thieves and robbers—have children and love them, receiving love in return—all except for me." He now thought like a simpleton without reason, similar to the childlike people he had become like.

He looked upon people differently than he had before. He was less shrewd, less proud, and instead was warmer, more curious, and more engaging. When he ferried ordinary travelers (childlike people, businessmen, warriors, or women), they did not seem as alien to him as they once had. He understood them and shared their lives, which were not guided by thoughts and insight, but only by urges and wishes. He felt akin to them. Even though he was close to perfection and was bearing his final wound, it still seemed to him as if these childlike people were his brothers. Their vanities, desires for possessions, and ridiculous traits were no longer laughable to him. They became comprehendible, lovable, and even worthy of veneration to him. All of the childish, simple, foolish, and yet very strong and vibrant urges and desires that prevailed among them—the blind love of a mother for her child, the stupid and blind pride of a conceited father for his only son, the blind and wild desire of a young, vain woman for jewelry and admiration from men—all of these desires were no longer childish to Siddhartha. He saw people live for themselves, saw

99

them achieve an infinite amount for themselves, saw them travel, wage war, suffer an infinite amount, and endure an infinite amount. He could love them for it, and he saw life and that which is alive—the indestructible Brahman—in each of their passions and actions. These people were worthy of love and admiration in their blind loyalty, strength, and tenacity. There was nothing they lacked, and there was nothing that the wise one or thinker possessed that put him above the rest of them except for one single, small, tiny thing: the awareness and conscious thought of the unity of all life. At many times, Siddhartha even doubted whether this knowledge should be so highly valued, or whether it was also perhaps some childishness of the intellectual people, the childlike people who practiced thinking. In every other regard, worldly people were of equal rank to the wise men, and were often far superior to them in the same way that animals can, in some moments, seem superior to humans because of the tough, unrelenting pursuit of necessities.

The realization and knowledge of what wisdom actually is slowly blossomed and ripened within Siddhartha; he now knew what the goal of his long search was. His goal was nothing more than a readiness of the soul, an ability and secret method of thinking the thought of unity every moment of his life, and being able to feel and inhale the unity. This is what blossomed within him and was shining back at him from Vasudeva's old, childlike face: harmony, knowledge of the eternal perfection of the world, smiles, and unity.

The wound still burned, however, and Siddhartha thought bitterly and longingly about his son. He nurtured love and tenderness in his heart, and allowed the pain to gnaw at him, and reveled in all the foolish acts of love. This flame would not go out on its own.

One day, when the wound was burning violently, Siddhartha crossed the river and was driven by a yearning. He got off the boat and wanted to go into the city and look for his son. The river flowed softly and quietly. It was the dry season, but the river's voice sounded strange: it laughed! It clearly laughed. The river laughed brightly and clearly at the old ferryman. Siddhartha stopped, bent over the water in order to hear the river better, and saw his face reflected in the quietly moving waters. In this reflected face was a reminder of something he had forgotten, and as he thought about it, he found it: this face resembled another face which he used to know, love, and fear. It resembled the face of his father, the Brahmin. He remembered how he, long ago when he was a young man, had forced his father to let him go to the penitents, and how he had said farewell to him, and how he had gone and never come back. Hadn't his father also suffered the same pain on his account that he was now suffering because of his son?

Hadn't his father long since died alone without having seen his son again? Didn't Siddhartha have to expect this same fate himself? Wasn't this repetition, this running around in fateful circles, a strange and stupid comedy?

The river laughed. Yes, it was so; everything that had not been suffered and come to its resolution returned again. The same pain was suffered time and time again. But Siddhartha went back to the boat and went back to the hut. He thought of his father, his son, and the river was laughing at him. He was at odds with himself: he was inclined to despair, and was no less inclined to laugh at himself and the entire world. Alas, the wound was not yet blossoming, and his heart still fought his fate. Good cheer and victory did not yet shine from his suffering. Nevertheless, he felt hope, and once he had returned to the hut, he felt and indefatigable desire to open up to Vasudeva, showing and saying everything to him who was the master of listening.

Vasudeva sat in the hut and wove a basket. He no longer used the ferry boat, as not only were his eyes starting to get weak, but his arms and hands were as well. The joy and cheerful benevolence of his face were the only things that were unchanged and flourishing.

Siddhartha sat down next to the old man and slowly began to talk. He now told him about that which they had never talked about: his walk to the city that one time, his burning wound, the envy he experienced at the sight of happy fathers, how he knew such wishes to be foolish, and how his fight against them was futile. He recounted everything, and he was able to say everything. Even the most embarrassing parts could be spoken; everything could be shown, everything told. He laid bare his wound, and told about how he fled today, going across the water in a childish sort of running away. He told how he was willing to walk to the city, and how the river had laughed.

Siddhartha spoke for a long time, and Vasudeva listened with a quiet face. Vasudeva's listening gave Siddhartha a sensation that was stronger than ever before. He sensed how his pain and fears flowed over to Vasudeva, and how the secret hope flowed over and came back to him from his companion. Showing his wound to this listener was just like bathing it in the river until it had cooled and become one with the river. While he was speaking, admitting and confessing all this, Siddhartha felt more and more that this was no longer Vasudeva, a human being, who was listening to him; he felt that this motionless listener was absorbing his confession into himself as a tree did the rain. He felt that this motionless man was the river itself, God himself, that he was eternity itself. While Siddhartha stopped thinking about himself and his wound, this realization of Vasudeva's changed nature took possession of him, and the more he felt it and entered into this nature, the less wondrous it became, and the more he realized that everything was in its proper place and natural. Vasudeva had already been like this for a long time—forever, almost—and Siddhartha was the only one who had not quite recognized it; yes, and he himself had almost reached the same state. He felt that he was now seeing old Vasudeva as the people see the gods, and that this could not last. In his heart, he began to say goodbye to Vasudeva. He talked incessantly through all of this.

When Siddhartha had finished talking, Vasudeva turned his friendly eyes, which had grown somewhat weak, directly at him. He said nothing, letting his silent love and cheer, his understanding and knowledge shine at him. He took Siddhartha's hand, led him to the seat by the riverbank, and sat down with him, smiling at the river.

"You've heard it laugh," he said. "But you haven't heard everything. Let's listen. You'll hear more."

They listened. The polyphonic song of the river resonated softly. Siddhartha looked into the water, and images appeared to him out of the moving water: his father appeared, and he was lonely and mourning for his son; he himself appeared, and he was also in bondage with yearning for his estranged son; his son appeared, and he was also lonely, as the boy greedily stormed along the burning road of his young wishes, reaching every goal, obsessed by every goal and every suffering. The river sang with a voice of suffering, and it sang longingly, flowing towards its goal. Its voice resonated with lamentations.

"Do you hear?" asked the mute gaze of Vasudeva. Siddhartha nodded.

"Listen closer!" whispered Vasudeva.

Siddhartha endeavored to listen better. The images of his father, himself, and his son merged. Kamala's image also appeared and was dispersed, and the images of Govinda and others merged with one another, all turning into the river, and all heading for the goal as the river itself. They were all filled with desire and suffering, and the river's voice was filled with yearning, burning woe, and unsatisfied desire. The river was headed for the goal, and Siddhartha saw it hurrying. The river, which consisted of him, his loved ones, and all the people he had ever seen, hurried in waves of suffering water towards many goals: the waterfall, the lake, the rapids, or the sea. Each goal was achieved, and every goal was followed by a new one as the water turned into vapor and rose into the sky, transformed then into rain and poured down from the sky, turned into a source, a stream, or a river, and then continued to flow onward once again. The longing voice, however, had changed. It still resounded with suffering and seeking, but other voices had joined it: voices of joy and suffering, good and evil, laughter or sadness. There were hundreds or even thousands of voices.

Siddhartha listened. He was nothing but a listener now; he was completely concentrated on listening, completely empty. He felt that he had now finished learning how to listen. He had often heard all of these many voices in the river before; today, however, they sounded new. He could no longer distinguish the individual voices in the multitude, could not differentiate between the happy ones and weeping ones, the children and the men. All the voices belonged together: the lamentation of yearning and the laughter of the wise one, the scream of rage and the moaning of the dying ones. All was one, and everything was intertwined and connected, entangled together a thousand times over. And together—all the voices, all the goals, all suffering, pleasure, good, and evil—together, it was all the world. All of it together was the flow of events and the music of life. And, when Siddhartha listened attentively to this river that contained the song of a thousand voices, when he listened neither to the suffering nor the laughter and did not bind his soul to any individual voice but submerged his self into it, and when he heard them all and perceived the entirety and the unity of it, then the great song of a thousand voices consisted of a single word, and that was "Om," the perfection.

"Do you hear?" asked Vasudeva's gaze again.

Vasudeva's smile was shining brightly, and floating radiantly over all the wrinkles of his old face just as the "Om" was floating in the air over all the voices of the river. His smile was shining brightly when he looked at his friend, and the same smile now started to shine brightly on Siddhartha's face as well. His wound now blossomed, and his suffering was radiant; his self had taken flight into the unity.

Siddhartha stopped fighting his fate this very hour, and he stopped suffering. Blooming on his face was mirth of a knowledge no longer opposed by any will, knowing perfection, and in agreement with the flow of events and the current of life. This mirth was full of sympathy for the pain and pleasure of others; it was devoted to the flow and dedicated to the unity.

When Vasudeva stood up from the seat by the riverbank and looked into Siddhartha's eyes, he saw the mirth and the knowledge shining within them. He then touched Siddhartha's shoulder softly with his hand, and in this careful and tender manner, he said: "I've been waiting for this hour, my friend. Now that it has come, let me leave. I've been waiting for this hour for a long time. I've been Vasudeva the ferryman for a long time. Now it has been long enough. Farewell, hut; farewell, river; farewell, Siddhartha!"

Siddhartha bowed deeply before the one who was bidding him farewell.

"I have known this would come," he said quietly. "You'll go into the forest?"

"I'm going into the forest; I'm entering the unity," spoke Vasudeva with a bright smile.

He left with this same bright smile, and Siddhartha watched him leave. Siddhartha watched him leave with deep joy and intense solemnity; he saw that Vasudeva's steps were full of peace, that his head was filled with radiance, and that his whole body was filled with light.

Govinda

DURING A PAUSE between pilgrimages, Govinda spent his time together with the other monks in the pleasure grove which the courtesan Kamala had given as a gift to the followers of Gotama. Govinda had heard rumors of an old ferryman, considered by many to be a wise man, who lived by the river one day's journey away. When Govinda continued his journey, he chose the path that went to the ferry. He was eager to see the ferryman because, even though he had followed the rules his entire life and was now looked upon with veneration by the younger monks because of his age and demeanor, the restlessness and seeking had not been extinguished in his heart.

He arrived at the river and asked the old man to ferry him over; when they got off the boat on the opposite bank, he said to the old man: "You're very kind to us monks and pilgrims, and you have already ferried many of us across the river. Aren't you also a seeker of the right path, ferryman?"

Siddhartha spoke, and a smile came from his old eyes: "Do you call yourself a seeker, O venerable one, although you are already advanced in years and are wearing the robe of Gotama's monks?"

"It's true; I'm old," said Govinda, "but I haven't stopped searching. I'll never stop searching; this seems to be my destiny. It seems to me that you, too, have been searching. Would you like to tell me something, O honorable one?"

Siddhartha spoke: "What could I possibly have to tell you, O venerable one? Perhaps only that you're doing far too much searching? That, in all your seeking, you don't make the time for finding?"

"How is that?" asked Govinda.

"When someone is searching," said Siddhartha, "then it can easily happen that the only thing his eyes see is that for which he is searching. He is then unable to find anything or let any thought enter his mind because he always thinks of nothing but the object of his search. He is obsessed by a goal; searching means having a goal. But finding means: being free, open, and having no goal. You, O venerable one, are perhaps indeed a seeker, because, in striving for your goal, there are many things that you don't see, even though they are right in front of your eyes."

"I don't quite understand yet," said Govinda. "What do you mean by this?"

Siddhartha said: "A long time ago, O venerable one—many years ago—you were once at this river and found there a man sleeping by it. You sat down with him to guard his sleep. But you, O Govinda, did not recognize the sleeper."

Astounded, like one who has just been spellbound, the monk looked into the ferryman's eyes.

"Are you Siddhartha?" he asked in a timid voice. "I wouldn't have recognized you this time, either! I greet you heartily, Siddhartha; I'm truly happy to see you once more! You've changed quite a bit, my friend—and you've now become a ferryman?"

Siddhartha laughed in a friendly way. "A ferryman, yes. Many people have to change a lot, Govinda. They have to wear many robes. I am one of these, my friend. I welcome you, Govinda, and invite you to spend the night in my hut."

Govinda stayed in the hut that night, sleeping on the bed which once was Vasudeva's. He posed many questions to the friend of his youth, and had Siddhartha tell him many things from his life.

When the time had come the next morning for Govinda to start the day's journey, he said these words without hesitation: "Before I go on my way, Siddhartha, permit me to ask one more question. Do you have a teaching? Do you have a faith or a knowledge that you follow which helps you to live and to do what is right?"

Siddhartha spoke: "You know, my friend, that as a young man when we lived with the penitents in the forest I was already wary of teachers and lessons, turning my back on them. I have stood by this position. Even so, I have had many teachers since then. A beautiful courtesan was my teacher for a long time, and a rich merchant was my teacher, and also some people who gambled with dice. Even a follower of Buddha who traveled on foot was once my teacher; he sat with me when I had fallen asleep in the forest on the pilgrimage. I've also learned from this river and from my predecessor, the ferryman Vasudeva. He was a very simple person, Vasudeva was, and he was no scholar, but he knew what is necessary just as well as Gotama did. He was a perfect man and a saint."

Govinda said: "Oh Siddhartha, you still enjoy mocking people a little bit, it seems to me. I believe in you, and I know that you haven't followed any teacher. But haven't you found something on your own? Even though you've found no teachings, you still discovered certain thoughts and insights, that are your own and help you to live. It would delight my heart if you were to tell me some of these."

Siddhartha spoke: "I've certainly had thoughts and insights, time and again. I have sometimes felt knowledge within me as one would feel life within one's heart for hours or days at a time. There have been many thoughts, but it would be difficult for me to transfer them to you. See here, Govinda, this is one of the thoughts that I've found: wisdom cannot be passed on. Wisdom that a wise man attempts to pass on to someone always sounds like foolishness."

"Are you joking?" asked Govinda.

"I'm not joking; I'm telling you what I've found. Knowledge can be transferred, but not wisdom. It can be found and lived, and it is possible to be carried by it. Miracles can be performed with it, but it can't be expressed and taught with words. This was what I sometimes suspected even as a young man, and what has driven me away from teachers. I have found another thought, Govinda, that you'll also regard as foolishness or a joke, but which is my best thought. It says: the opposite of every truth is just as true! That is to say, any truth can only be expressed and put into words when it is one-sided. Everything that can be thought with the mind and said with words is one-sided, it's all just the half of it, lacking complete-ness, roundness, or unity. When the exalted Gotama spoke his teachings about the world, he had to divide it into Samsara and Nirvana,† deception and truth, suffering and salvation. It can't be done any differently, and there is no other way for the person who wants to teach. But the world itself that exists around us and inside of us is never one-sided. A person or an action is never entirely Samsara or Nirvana, and a person is never completely holy or sinful. It really seems like this, of course, because we are subject to the deception that time is something real. Time is not real, Govinda; I have experienced this many times over. And if time is not real, then the divide which seems to separate the world from eternity, suffering from bliss, and evil from good, is also a deception."

"How is that?" asked Govinda timidly.

"Listen well, my friend; listen well! The sinner—as I am and you are—is a sinner, but in time he will come to be Brahman again. In time,

he will reach Nirvana and will be Buddha, and these "times to come" are
only a deception and a parable! The sinner is not on his way to becoming
a Buddha and is not in the process of developing, even though our capac-
ity for thought does not know how else to envision these things. No, the
future Buddha is within the sinner now; his future is already completely
there today. One has to worship within oneself, in you, and in everyone
else the Buddha that is coming into being, that is possible: the hidden
Buddha. The world, my friend Govinda, is not imperfect or on a slow path
towards perfection; no, it is perfect every moment. All sin already carries
divine forgiveness within itself, all small children already have the old
person within themselves, all infants have death, all the dying have eternal
life. It isn't possible for any one person to see how far another one has
already progressed on his path, because the Buddha is waiting inside the
robber and the gambler, and the robber is waiting within the Brahmin. It is
also possible through deep meditation to put time out of existence and to
see all the life that was and is and ever will be as if they were all simultane-
ous; in that simultaneity is everything that is good, perfect, and Brahman.
I therefore see whatever exists as good. Death is like life to me, sin is like
holiness, wisdom is like foolishness; everything has to be just as it is, and
everything requires only my consent, willingness, and loving agreement
to become good to me and work for my benefit, unable to ever harm me.
I have experienced a great deal of sin in my body and soul that I needed;
I needed lust, the desire for possessions, vanity, and the most shameful
despair in order to learn how to surrender all resistance, love the world,
and stop comparing it to some kind of world that I imagined or wished
for—a perfection that I had dreamed up. I had to learn how to leave the
world as it is, to love it, and to enjoy being a part of it. These, oh Govinda,
are some of the thoughts that have come into my mind.

Siddhartha bent down, picked a stone up from the ground, and
weighed it in his hand.

"This here," he said playfully "is a stone. It will, after a certain time,
perhaps turn into soil, and from soil it will turn into a plant, animal, or
human being. In the past, I would have said: 'This stone is just a stone;
it is worthless and it belongs to the world of the Maya. And yet, because
it might be able to become a human being and a spirit in the cycle of
transformation, I also grant that it is important.' This is how I might have
thought in the past. But today, I think that this stone is a stone, and it is
also an animal, a god, and Buddha; I do not venerate it because it could
turn into this or that, but rather because it already is and always will be
everything. The very fact that it is a stone and appears to me today and

now as a stone is the reason why I love it and see worth and purpose in each of its veins and cavities, in the yellow and gray, in the hardness, in the sound it makes when I knock at it, or in the dryness or wetness of its surface. There are stones which feel like oil or soap, and others that feel like leaves or sand. Every one is special and prays to the "Om" in its own way, and each one is Brahman, but at the same time they are just as much a stone, and are oily or juicy, and it is this very fact that I like and regard as wondrous or worthy of worship. But I won't speak any more of this. These words are not sufficient for this secret meaning. Everything always comes out a little differently as soon as it is put into words. It gets distorted slightly and seems a bit silly—yes, this is also very good and I like it quite a bit, and I agree with the idea that what is one man's treasure and wisdom always sounds like foolishness to someone else."

Govinda listened silently.

"Why did you tell me about this stone?" he asked hesitantly after a pause.

"I did so without any specific intention. Or perhaps I intended to say that I love this stone, and the river, and all the things at which we are looking and from which we can learn. I can love a stone, Govinda, as well as a tree or a piece of bark. These are things, and things can be loved. But I cannot love words. Teachings, therefore, are no good to me. They have no hardness or softness, no colors, edges, odor, or taste; they have nothing but words. Perhaps it is these many words which keep you from finding peace. In the same vein, salvation and virtue as well as Samsara and Nirvana are merely words, Govinda. There is nothing that could become Nirvana—there is only the word Nirvana."

Govinda spoke: "Nirvana is not just a word, my friend. It is an idea."

Siddhartha continued: "It might be a thought, that's true. I have to confess to you, my friend, that I don't differentiate much between thoughts and words. To be honest, I don't have a high opinion of thoughts, either. I have a better opinion of things. Here on this ferry boat, for instance, a holy man who for many years believed simply in the river, and nothing else, has been my predecessor and teacher. He noticed that the river spoke to him and he learned from it. It educated him and taught him; the river seemed to be a god to him, and for many years he did not know that every wind, cloud, bird, and beetle was just as divine, knows just as much, and can teach just as much as the reverent river. When this holy man went into the forest, however, he knew everything. Without teachers or books, he knew more than you and I do—only because he had believed in the river.

Govinda said: "But is that which you call 'things' actually real; is it something which has existence? Isn't it just an image or illusion—a deception of the Maya? Is your stone, your tree, or your river actually a reality?"

"I don't care very much about this, either," said Siddhartha. "They may be illusions, and they may not be; after all, I would be an illusion, too, and in any case they are always as I am. This is what makes them so dear to me and worthy of veneration: they are like me, and, therefore, I can love them. This is another teaching that you will laugh about: love, O Govinda, seems to me to be the most important thing of all. Great thinkers may try to thoroughly understand the world, explain it, and despise it. But I'm only interested in being able to love the world, not despise it. I don't want to hate it and have it hate me; I want to be able to look upon it and myself and upon all beings with love, admiration, and great respect."

"I understand this," said Govinda. "This very thing, however, was discovered by the exalted one to be a deception. He commands us to be benevolent, forgiving, sympathetic, and tolerant—but not to love. He forbade us from binding our hearts to earthly things with love."

"I know that," said Siddhartha. His smile shone like gold. "I know that, Govinda. Behold, with that we are now right in the middle of the thicket of opinions, disputing over words. I can't deny that my words about love seem to contradict Gotama's words. It's for this very reason that I mistrust words so much, because I know this contradiction is a deception. I know that I am in agreement with Gotama. How could he, who has discovered all elements of human existence to be transitory and meaningless and yet still loved people so much, using his long, laborious life only to help and teach them—how could he not know love? Even with him, your great teacher, I prefer the thing itself to the words, and place more importance on his actions and life than on his speeches, more stock in the gestures of his hand than in his opinions. I see his greatness not in his speech or his thoughts, but only in his actions and life."

The two old men said nothing for a long time. Then Govinda spoke while he was bowing in farewell: "Thank you, Siddhartha, for telling me some of your thoughts. They are somewhat strange thoughts, and it hasn't all been immediately understandable. Be this as it may, I thank you and I wish you peaceful days."

(Secretly, however, Govinda thought to himself: This Siddhartha is a strange person. He articulates odd ideas and his teachings sound foolish. They sound so different from the exalted one's pure lessons, which are clearer, purer, more understandable. Nothing strange, foolish, or silly is contained within them. But Siddhartha's hands, feet, eyes, forehead, breath, smile, greeting, and gait seemed different from his ideas. I have not seen since our exalted Gotama became one with the Nirvana a person of whom I could say: 'this is a holy man!' I have found only Siddhartha to be like this. His teachings may be strange and his words may sound foolish, but a purity, calmness, mirth, mildness, and holiness that I have found in no one else since our exalted teacher's death shines out of his gaze, hands, skin, and hair.)

While Govinda thought these things, there was a conflict within his heart. Drawn by love, he once again bowed to Siddhartha. He bowed deeply to the one who was sitting calmly.

"Siddhartha," he said, "we have become old men. It is unlikely that we will see each other again in this incarnation. I see, my beloved friend, that you have found peace. I confess that I have not found this. Tell me one more word, oh honorable one; give me something as I go on my way which I can grasp and understand! Give me something that will be with me along my path. My path is often dark and difficult, Siddhartha."

Siddhartha said nothing, and looked at Govinda with his quiet smile that never changed. Govinda stared at his face with fear, yearning, and suffering. The eternal search and endless not-finding was visible in his look.

Siddhartha saw it and smiled.

"Bend down to me!" he whispered quietly in Govinda's ear. Bend down to me! Like this, but even closer! Very close! Kiss my forehead, Govinda!"

Drawn by great love and expectation, Govinda obeyed these words with astonishment. But while he bent down close to Siddhartha and touched his forehead with his lips, something miraculous happened to him. While his thoughts still dwelled on Siddhartha's strange words, and while he struggled in vain and with reluctance to banish time with his thoughts and imagine Nirvana and Samsara as one, and while certain contempt for his friends' words was fighting within him against an immense love and veneration, the following happened to him:

He saw the face of his friend Siddhartha no longer, but instead saw a long sequence of many other faces—a flowing river of hundreds or thousands of faces—all come and disappear, and yet seem to be there simultaneously. The faces were constantly changing and renewing themselves, and yet they were all still Siddhartha. He saw the face of a fish—a carp—with a mouth opened in unending pain. It was the face of a dying fish, with fading eyes. He saw the face of a newborn babe that was red, full of wrinkles, and distorted with crying. He saw the face of a murderer, and saw him plunging a knife into someone else's body. In the same instant, he saw this criminal in bondage, kneeling while his head was chopped off with one blow from the executioner's sword. He saw the naked bodies of men and women in positions and struggles of frenzied love. He saw corpses that were stretched out, cold, motionless, and empty. He saw the heads of various animals: boars, crocodiles, elephants, bulls, and birds. He saw gods: Krishna† and Agni.† He saw all these figures and faces in a thousand relationships with one another, helping, loving, hating, destroying, or giving birth again to each other. Each one had a will to die, and a passionate, painful recognition of ephemerality—and yet none of them did die, they were only transformed, and were always reborn. They eternally received a new face, without any time passing between the one face and the next, and all of these figures and faces rested, flowed, and conceived themselves. They floated along and merged with one another, and they were always covered with something thin that had no nature of its own but nonetheless existed—like thin glass or ice, a transparent skin, mold, or mask of water. This mask was smiling, and this mask was Siddhartha's smiling face, which Govinda touched with his lips at this very same moment. And Govinda saw that the smile of this mask, the smile of unity on the flowing forms, the smile of coexistence in the thousand births and deaths, the smile of Siddhartha, was exactly the same type of smile as the quiet, delicate, impenetrable, wise, sometimes-benevolent, sometimes-mocking, thousand-fold smile of Gotama, the Buddha, as he himself had looked upon it with reverence a hundred times. Govinda knew that perfected ones smiled like this.

Not knowing any more whether time existed, whether the vision had lasted a second or a hundred years, not knowing any more whether there existed a Siddhartha, a Gotama, a me and a you, feeling in his innermost self as if he had been wounded by a divine arrow, the injury of which tasted sweet, being transformed by magic and dissolved in his innermost self, Govinda still stood for a bit while bent over the quiet face of Siddhartha, which he had just kissed and which had just been the scene of all manifestations, all transformations, all existence. This countenance was unchanged, and after the depth of that thousand-fold face had subsided beneath the surface, Siddhartha smiled silently, quietly, and softly. It was perhaps benevolent, perhaps mocking, and was precisely like the exalted one used to smile.

Govinda bowed deeply. Tears coming from he knew not where ran down his old face, and a feeling of the most intimate love and most humble veneration burned like a fire in his heart. He bowed deeply and touched the ground before the one who was sitting motionlessly and whose smile reminded him of everything he had ever loved and everything that had ever been valuable and holy to him in his life.

Glossary

<u>First Part</u>
<u>The Son of the Brahmin</u>

Brahmin – the class of priests in Hindu society; a member of this society. This class is the highest of the four Hindu castes (see note: *caste* in "With the Samanas" glossary).

sala – a type of hardwood tree with resin that is used for incense, for caulking boats, and for lamp fuel; it is said that the Buddha died underneath one of these trees.

"Om" – a mystical, religious Hindu word, which is said to embody the universal spirit; it is a word regularly chanted during religious ceremonies to achieve a state of bliss.

Atman – [*Sanskrit*] "breath"; "individual soul"

Rig-Veda – the oldest religious scripture in the Hindu religion; this is the holiest of the four Hindu texts written between 1500 and 500 B.C. *Veda* refers to the collection of texts or verses that creates a body of knowledge from the original time period of the Hindu religion.

Prajapati – [*Sanskrit*] "author/protector of life"

Upanishads – a set of texts, the name of which indicates that it supposedly "removes ignorance by revealing knowledge of the universal spirit."

Sama-Veda – [*Sanskrit*] *Sama* means "ritual chant," and *Veda* means "knowledge"; the Sama-Veda (Samaveda) ranks third in level of importance in the four Hindu scriptures.

Brahman – related to the expansion of the soul that leads to knowledge of the universal spirit; it also refers to the spirit itself that sustains the universe. Note that *Brahman* is not the same as *Brahmin* (see note: *Brahmin*).

Satyam – [*Sanskrit*] "pure," "true"; that which lies beyond the illusion of the world.

Samanas – [*Sanskrit*] "to become weary or exhausted through effort"; in this context, the term is referring to those people who embody this attribute and practice severe self-discipline and self-denial.

<u>With the Samanas</u>

Nirvana – Nirvana represents a state of bliss that supposedly occurs when all personal desires have been eliminated, one's individual self is extinguished, and a person realizes that the soul and the universal spirit are one and the same.

caste – a social class; a segment of a divided society that is based on birth, wealth, and/or occupation. In Indian and Hindu societies, the four castes are (in order of importance) priests, warriors/administrators, merchants, and slaves. Below these are the "untouchables," who are essentially not a part of society and are considered "non-persons." The rigidity of the caste system has gradually relaxed since Hesse's time, but it is still strictly practiced and adhered to in many areas of Indian society.

Gotama
—

Awakening
Yoga-Veda – a word Hesse created to mean "knowledge of the practice of yoga"; *yoga* is the exercise/philosophy whose purpose is to unite one's self with the universal spirit.

Mara – the destroyer of Buddha and his religion, the evil one, the temptress, the seducer; the essence of Mara's temptations is worldly pleasure and desire.

Maya – [*Sanskrit*] "the illusion of the physical world"; Maya is essentially the world as it exists and is perceived by human beings.

Second Part
Kamala
Vishnu – the member of the Hindu trinity of gods (Brahma, Vishnu, Shiva) who sustains and preserves life.

Lakshmi – a goddess of fortune and beauty

With the Childlike People
—

Samsara
Samsara – [*Sanskrit*] "cycle of mundane life"; the idea means existing within the illusion of the world.

By the River
—

The Ferryman

—

The Son

—

"Om"

—

Govinda

Krishna – a Hindu god believed to be the eighth reincarnation of Vishnu (see note: *Vishnu* in the "Kamala" glossary above)

Agni – the Hindu god of fire who is worshipped as the guardian of all humanity

Vocabulary

First Part
The Son of the Brahmin
allay – to calm, alleviate
ascetics – people who practice self-denial to attain spiritual strength
gaunt – thin and slender, sometimes due to malnourishment
hawking – selling or advertising by shouting loudly in public places
illustrious – famous, brilliant, or dignified
plebian – of or relating to the lower class
raffia – a type of palm tree that gives fibers suitable for weaving
Sanskrit – the ancient language of India and Hinduism; all the Hindu Vedas
    (scriptures) were originally written in Sanskrit.
vacuous – shallow and devoid of intelligence
venerable – worthy of honor or respect

With the Samanas
adulation – adoration, reverence
anesthetic – a substance used to make one numb and/or drowsy
carrion – rotting flesh that is fed upon by animals
causality – the relationship between a cause and its effect
clarion – very clear and loud
decorum – proper and appropriate behavior or manners
dissolution – disintergration; destruction
feigned – pretended or gave the appearance of
gleaned – gathered
ineffable – indescribable; unable to be put into words
languished – became weak, faint, or discouraged
reciprocated – repaid; returned an action in kind and degree
sublime – of or belonging to an exalted spiritual state
tutelage – teaching, influence, guidance
visage – one's face; a facial expression
wafted – drifted on the air (usually in reference to odors)
zealous – fervent, passionate

Gotama
equanimity – remaining calm under stress
gait – a way of walking
imperceptible – unable to be sensed or seen
inscrutable – difficult to understand
insubstantial – lacking substance or significance; unimportant

Awakening
—

Second Part
Kamala
ablutions – ceremonial cleansings or washings

benefactor – one who helps or gives a gift to another (usually in a financial manner)

courtesan – a prostitute who serves the wealthy class

disembarking – getting out of a vehicle or ship

self-castigation – self-punishment, usually in a severe manner

With the Childlike People
destitute – without money or possessions

encomium – an expression of enthusiastic praise

myriad – a great number; numerous and of a wide variety

opulent – very wealthy; lavish

supple – able to bend and twist without breaking

Samsara
accolades – praises, recommendations

aspirations – hopes, dreams, goals

astutely – wisely, sagaciously

countenance – the expression on one's face

ensorcellment – placed under a spell; being in a trance

By the River
corporeal – relating to the body

ephemeral – temporary, transitional, fleeting

ignominious – dishonorable, shameful, humiliating

miser – a person who spends very little

The Ferryman
incessantly – without ceasing; constantly

The Son
abominable – horrific; worthy of scorn or revulsion

amiability – cheerfulness, friendliness

camaraderie – friendliness and good will toward companions

vacillation – the act or state of being indecisive or fickle

<u>"Om"</u>
indefatigable – not able to be tired or worn out
polyphonic – consisting of many tones or voices
tenacity – brave persistence

<u>Govinda</u>
—

Insightful and Reader-Friendly, Yet Affordable

Prestwick House Literary Touchstone Classic Editions–
The Editions By Which All Others May Be Judged

Every *Prestwick House Literary Touchstone Classic* is enhanced with Reading Pointers for Sharper Insight to improve comprehension and provide insights that will help students recognize key themes, symbols, and plot complexities. In addition, each title includes a Glossary of the more difficult words and concepts.

For the Shakespeare titles, along with the Reading Pointers and Glossary, we include margin notes and various strategies to understanding the language of Shakespeare.

New titles are constantly being added; call or visit our website for current listing.

Special Educator's Discount – At Least

50% Off